CORPSE AT
CAPTAIN'S SEAT

AND THEN THERE WERE SOME...

At long last, the renovations of stately Captain's Seat are mostly complete!

To celebrate, mystery bookseller and sometimes amateur sleuth Ellery Page decides to throw a house-warming party and invite his New York theater friends to stay for the weekend.

When a freak snowstorm leaves the house party cut off from the village of Pirate's Cove, there's nothing to do but drink, reminisce, and play games.

Or so Ellery thinks—until he finds himself trapped in a real-life game of Clue.

CORPSE AT

CAPTAIN'S SEAT

SECRETS & SCRABBLE BOOK EIGHT

JOSH LANYON

VELLICHOR BOOKS

An imprint of JustJoshin Publishing, Inc.

CORPSE AT CAPTAIN'S SEAT: AN M/M COZY MYSTERY
(Secrets and Scrabble Book 8)
July 2024

Published in the United States of America

JustJoshin Publishing, Inc.
3053 Rancho Vista Blvd.
Suite 116
Palmdale, CA 93551
www.joshlanyon.com

This is a work of fiction. Sadly, any resemblance to persons living or dead is entirely coincidental.

CHAPTER ONE

"*Another* secret passage?" Ellery Page, owner and proprietor of Pirate Cove's only mystery bookshop, balanced the phone receiver between his cheek and shoulder as he hurried to finish the Crow's Nest's payroll. With house guests arriving for the weekend, he was in a rush to wrap things up within the next hour so he could get over to the ferry landing.

"We can't be sure unless we open the wall up," Tony Brambilla, Ellery's contractor, was saying.

Brambilla and Sons had managed to pull off something close to a miracle as they'd worked to finish renovations on Captain's Seat before the winter—and Ellery's guests—set in. When Ellery had inherited the dilapidated 18th century mansion after the death of his Great-aunt Eudora nine months earlier, the place had been just about ready for the wrecking ball. A recent fire on the second floor had not helped matters.

Ellery said quickly, "No! Don't open any walls. My friends are arriving on the one o'clock ferry."

"All righty. Well, that door on the leeward side bedroom no longer sticks and the loose floorboards on the staircase have been repaired. If there *is* a passage behind that master bedroom wall, it probably connects to the tunnel opening onto the library."

During the extensive renovations, no less than two separate secret passages had been discovered within the walls of Captain's Seat. That was not unusual for the oldest buildings on an island that had once served as a pirate hideout. However, as exciting as was the sound of *secret passages*, the walkways inside Captain's Seat had turned out to be dank, dark tunnels filled with empty broken crates, spiders—one of Ellery's least favorite things—and not much else. One day he'd get around to fully exploring those interior alleys, but they were low priority. After all, he'd happily lived nearly a year in the old mansion without even realizing they were there.

"Enjoy your house," Tony was saying. "In the spring, we can talk about tackling those structural cracks in the cellar."

Ellery's heart sank at the words *structural cracks*, but he said with determined good cheer, "Yes. Thanks for all your hard work, Tony. Captain's Seat is like a different house." A house not in imminent peril of spontaneously combusting every time he flipped a light switch.

"It's good to have Pages on the island again."

That sentiment seemed to be broadly held in Pirate's Cove, but it still surprised and touched Ellery. Prior to inheriting Captain's Seat, he hadn't even known Buck Island existed—let alone his Great-aunt Eudora.

He ended the phone call with Tony, firmly blocking out all thoughts of structural cracks. He was just finishing up the payroll as the shop door's bells chimed in welcome and Nora Sweeney, his assistant manager, returned from lunch.

Nora was a wisp of a woman, just over five feet in her sensible shoes. Her eyes were the color of steel and she wore her long gray hair in a severe ponytail. Though prone to gossip and wild flights of imagination, she was clever, loyal, and boundlessly energetic. In addition to her vast knowledge of the island and all its inhabitants (past and present),

Nora possessed an encyclopedic knowledge of mystery, which had proved beyond valuable to Ellery. Before inheriting the Crow's Nest, he'd had zero interest in crime, either real or fictional.

What a difference a few months could make!

Watson, Ellery's black spaniel-mix puppy, hopped down from the long wooden library bench where he had been gazing solemnly out the picture windows at the empty cobblestone streets.

Pirate's Cove in November looked suspiciously like a ghost town, right down to the eerie tendrils of white mist winding around hanging signs and plant urns and porch columns. It was hard to remember that just two months earlier, tourists had crowded the streets, buzzing around in rented golf carts and filling up the beaches, shops, and cafés. Filling up local cash registers as well.

Nora stooped to pat Watson. "Looks like we're going to have snow this weekend," she announced.

"You're kidding." Ellery went to the windows, gazing out at the ominous leaden skies and white-capped harbor. Granted, ominous was normal for this time of year. "A lot of snow?"

Nora unwound her long red scarf. "I shouldn't think so, dearie. Not this early in the season. February's the worst month for snow. This time of year, we won't see much beyond a little powder. It'll provide local color for your guests."

"Right." He was already regretting his decision not to invest in a backup generator. But money only stretched so far, and the roof, plumbing, and electrical wiring had taken precedence.

Nora joined him at the windows, musing, "I hope your friends won't have too rough a crossing."

Yikes. "Me, too."

For a moment or two they watched the wind gusting across the waves, rocking the scattered boats in the harbor.

Yes, the island could be a bit desolate this time of year.

As though reading Ellery's mind, Nora said, "I don't suppose they'll be all that interested in outdoor activities anyway."

"No. True." Ellery glanced down at Watson, who wagged his tail hopefully. "Let me finish up a few things, buddy. Then we'll go for a you-know-what." To Nora, he said, "Tony Brambilla says they think they've discovered another hidden passageway, but they can't be sure without opening the wall up."

Nora's eyes kindled with excitement. "That makes sense. Captain's Seat is nearly as old as the Pirate Eight."

The Pirate Eight were the first manor houses built on Buck Island. All eight homes had started out as pirate fortresses.

"Why would Captain Horatio Page have needed a bunch of secret passages? He wasn't a pirate. He was a pirate hunter."

"True, a pirate hunter surrounded by pirates."

Ellery considered that cryptic remark as he returned to his office to make sure he hadn't left anything pressing undone. This was the first long weekend he'd taken since moving to the island—not counting two weeks of convalescing from a concussion sustained while snooping.

As he was checking his email one final time, Jack phoned.

Jack Carson was Pirate Cove's chief of police and Ellery's boyfriend—in fact, he was now Ellery's fiancé. A delightful fact Ellery was still getting used to.

"Hi, what time are you heading over to the ferry?"

Ellery glanced distractedly at the clock. "Two. Are you going to be able to get away tonight?"

"That's the plan," Jack said. "Do you need me to bring anything or—?"

"No. Just you."

Jack made a sound of amusement. "I think I can manage that. How many of your old crew are arriving this afternoon?"

"Flip, Tosh, Lenny, and Chelsea. Tomorrow we've got Oscar, Freddie, and Belle."

"Okay. And Tosh and Freddie used to be married?" That was quintessential Jack, making sure he had the cast of characters straight. Jack was not a play-it-by-ear guy. He was a show-up- on-time-and-know-your-lines guy.

"Correct."

"But that's not going to be awkward because it was a long time ago and everyone is over it."

"Right. Hopefully."

"And Belle and Oscar used to date, but now she's dating an English peer."

It sounded kind of ridiculous when Jack put it like that, but was nonetheless accurate.

"Yes."

"And you're confident we're going to get through the weekend without them killing each other because they haven't killed each other yet."

Ellery spluttered a laugh. "Something like that. I mean, it's all ancient history."

"Yeah, why doesn't that reassure me?" Jack sounded wry. "Have you seen the weather report for the weekend?"

"Nora says it's going to snow."

"She's not the only one. You might want to chop some extra firewood. Just in case."

That was a good thought—and so very Jack.

Ellery said, "Will do. Anyway, getting snowed in could be fun."

"Getting snowed in could be very fun, although probably less fun with a crowd."

Ellery's mouth curved. "I can't argue with that. But we'll have other snow days." He could say that now with confidence.

"That we will," Jack said, and Ellery could hear the smile in his voice.

The sea surrounding Buck Island was more than a body of water. For centuries that mysterious deep had created a barricade against the outside world and shaped the character of the islanders. It remained a constant presence, hovering on the edge of the island's every interaction. The sound of it filled the dark nights; its blue shadow provided the backdrop of every single day.

As Ellery waited for the ferry, he could taste salt on the raw east wind, smell that briny broth as the winter-rough water tumbled and roiled golden strands of seaweed. A clammy dampness clung to his skin. Watson repeatedly shook himself as though trying to rid himself of the biting mist.

The ferry was late by nearly twenty minutes, and when it finally docked, only a handful of slightly green passengers stumbled down the gangplank. Most of them seemed to be Ellery's friends.

"*Ellery*!" Tosh waved to him, towing Lenny along.

"Ahoy!" Ellery waved back. "Welcome to Pirate's Cove!"

Tosh and Lenny were followed by Flip, who looked like a well-groomed ghost (right down to the phosphorescent tinge of his face) and Chelsea, huffing and puffing as she dragged a mountain of luggage behind her.

Watson, who had never met any of these people in his brief life, nonetheless began to bark as though he'd spotted long-lost comrades.

Arf! Arf! Arf!

"Oh, my gosh, he's SO cute!" Tosh's voice rang across the water.

Unsurprisingly, Tosh—a tall, red-haired and boundlessly energetic young woman—seemed the least bothered by what had clearly been a rough trip from Point Judith.

Ellery started down the concrete walkway, and everyone spent the next few minutes hugging and kissing hello.

"I can't believe you're finally here," Ellery told them.

Arf! Arf! Arf! Watson seconded.

"Same," Lenny moaned. "If I'd realized we had to round flipping Cape Horn—"

Tosh cut her off. "Ell, you look terrific! You're like a walking ad for Ralph Lauren. Here, take Lenny before she falls into the harbor. Our luggage is still onboard."

Ellery stopped hugging Flip—Phillip Daly to talent agents and casting directors—in order to receive Lenny, or "Goth Girl" as they'd referred to her back in the day. Lenny was small and wiry with black-green hair and wide green eyes. *Usually,* her eyes were wide. At the moment, they showed a tendency to roll back in her head.

"*Ugh,*" Lenny moaned, and sank through Ellery's hold in order to sit on the cement. "Another three minutes and I'd have thrown myself overboard."

"That happens a lot in these parts." He moved to help Chelsea with the tower of suitcases she was attempting to haul single-handedly up the walkway. He called after Tosh, "Wait. Isn't this your luggage?"

Flip and Lenny laughed. "That's just Chelsea's gear," Flip told Ellery.

"Hey, I'm past the age of living out of a knapsack," Chelsea snapped.

Ellery did a doubletake. Not at the luggage. At Chelsea.

Chelsea was, without question, the most gifted actor in their clique, but off-stage she had always made a point of scorning any kind of (her word) *artifice*. She was average height, average weight and, regardless of the season, preferred to dress in jeans and flannel shirts. As long as Ellery had known her, she'd worn her lank brown hair to her shoulders and avoided any makeup more elaborate than sunscreen. But now?

Now Chelsea's brown hair was stylishly cut and gilded with coppery highlights. She wore lash extensions and had clearly had lip injections. Like Tosh, she wore combat boots, jeans, and a black parka that, except for the color, looked exactly like Tosh's teal one.

"Wow. Chelsea. I almost didn't recognize you behind all those suitcases."

Chelsea knew exactly what he meant. Her smile was sour. "Is that supposed to be a compliment?"

"And that's just her hair products," Flip put in.

Chelsea made a face at him. "Ha. Ha."

"Help," Lenny moaned. She was now flat on the cement as Watson worked frantically to deliver mouth-to-mouth resuscitation.

Ellery abandoned Chelsea's luggage and went to rescue Lenny. He scooped up Watson who, knowing his life-saving work was not done, objected loudly. An elderly seagull perched on the white railing was offended by such language, and began to offer his views.

The remaining passengers straggling off the ferry gave their impromptu theatrical production wide berth.

"Where are you parked, Ell?" Flip hauled Lenny to her feet.

"It's the navy-blue VW behind the snack bar. I think we can all squeeze in, but I hired a taxi to bring your luggage to the house."

"You didn't have to do that." Chelsea looked more uneasy than relieved.

But yeah, unless Ellery wanted to make several trips to and from the ferry landing, he had to do that. "Common procedure. No worries. Ezra won't lose your luggage."

Chelsea looked unconvinced.

Lenny, half-draped over Flip's shoulder, said, "Someone should tell Ell about the escaped maniac."

Naturally, Ellery laughed. Chelsea said, "You only think she's kidding."

"Here's Tosh," Flip said, and they all turned to watch Tosh ably steering two large suitcases down the gangplank. The wheels of the luggage thumped noisily on the aluminum and carbon fiber ramp.

Watson, firmly clamped beneath Ellery's arm, wriggled to get down, shouting enthusiastic greetings, as though Tosh had just returned from an overseas voyage.

"Did you tell him about the homicidal maniac?" Tosh was only slightly out of breath as she rejoined them.

Ellery laughed again.

"He doesn't believe us," Lenny said.

Flip said, "Yeah, but really."

"Oh, come *on*."

Tosh shook her fiery hair back, saying earnestly, "No, Ell, listen. When we got to the ferry terminal there were all these cop cars with flashing lights. We asked what was going on, and one of the officers said a patient had escaped from the Rhode Island State Psychiatric Hospital, and that they had reason to believe he was going to try to get to Buck Island."

Ellery rolled his eyes. "Okay. Sure. Do they call him the Cat?"

"What?" Tosh was confused. She looked at Flip.

"Or does he have a hook for a hand?"

Flip huffed, but insisted, "We're not making this up."

"Okay, maybe it's a mass hallucination. All that fresh air at once could be dangerous for you city folk."

"City folk?" retorted Tosh. "Who are you supposed to be? Rilla of the Lighthouse?"

Ellery laughed.

"Okay, but seriously," Lenny said. "And then once we boarded, the crew came around and checked all our tickets again."

"Well, there you go," Ellery said. "We all know the only reason to collect tickets is to prevent homicidal maniacs from enjoying free rides."

"Okay, but there weren't that many passengers. And after they checked our tickets, the crew started searching the boat. They were trying to pretend it was standard procedure, but come on! They were checking the lifejacket storage bins. They were obviously looking for someone who shouldn't have been on board."

Chelsea said, "We're not saying he actually got *on* the boat. Just that they were obviously worried he might have."

Flip said, "I know it sounds like one of those spooky campfire tales, but—"

It seemed some things never changed.

Ellery was half-amused, half-exasperated. "You know, it's not like I've forgotten we did *The Cat and the Can*ary at Tisch."

Flip, Tosh, Lenny, and Chelsea all looked at each other with varying degrees of blankness.

Ellery prompted, "Eccentric Uncle Cyrus dies and leaves his estate to his niece Annabelle with the stipulation she has to spend the night in the creepy family mansion, but then when Annabelle and the other heirs arrive at Haunted Hollow, they're stalked by a mysterious figure they believe to be the Cat, an escapee from the local asylum who's hiding out in the secret passages." He had to stop for breath. "I *know* you remember. Flip was the Cat and Noah played Uncle Cyrus."

Noah. Wow. He felt a pang at that memory.

"Noah. That's right," Flip murmured.

"*Oh.*" Tosh looked startled. "I do remember. I played Annabelle. You were Charlie."

"You were *terrible*," Chelsea informed Ellery.

"I know."

Tosh said vaguely, "Noah. God." She glanced at Lenny, who was frowning at the ferry as if still waiting for a final passenger to disembark.

Ellery uneasily studied the *Pirate Que*en, rocking back and forth in her mooring.

Was something going on? There seemed to be a lot of serious-faced conferencing going on between the crew members gathered at the stern of the ship.

"I'm pretty sure you're the only one who even remembers that production," Tosh said. "But even if it is a funny coincidence, why on earth would we make up a story like this?"

"Why would you Saran-wrap me to the sofa?"

Tosh and Lenny started giggling. Flip looked slightly guilty. Chelsea said, "We didn't want your next performance to be stale."

"Why would you pose a demon mannequin in my closet? Why would you—"

Flip interrupted, "Okay, yes, we *all* love practical jokes. Let's not forget, you're the one who put that demon mannequin in my *bed*."

"Oh, that was brilliant!" Tosh exclaimed. "They heard your scream all the way over in Manhattan."

Flip made a face at her.

"You put a fake tarantula in my oatmeal!" Ellery was laughing, though. They were all laughing.

"Oops. That was me," Chelsea admitted. "I lied about it being Flip's idea."

"Anyway," Flip said, "Your boyfriend's the chief of police, right? Why not ask *him*?"

CHAPTER TWO

"**A**ctually…" Jack said.

"*What*?" Ellery yelped. "Are you seriously telling me there's a homicidal maniac on the loose?"

Ellery was back in his office at the Crow's Nest. Flip, Tosh, Lenny, and Chelsea had insisted they wanted to see the bookshop before driving out to Captain's Seat. He could hear them—everyone talking at once per usual—and Nora and Kingston's bemused answers. He waited for Jack's careful reply.

Jack was always honest, so the carefulness was the point.

"*Maniac* isn't a clinical term. Last night a court-ordered forensic patient did escape the state psychiatric hospital on the Cranston campus. There's a possibility he might try to make his way to the island. But that's all it is. A possibility. There's no reason to believe he's already on the island."

"What did this court-ordered forensic patient, who might or might not be headed our way, do to get himself committed?"

Jack sighed.

"Okay. *That*. That sigh. *That* is worrying."

"There's nothing to worry about," Jack said in a tone that could best be described as professionally soothing.

"Because this escaped patient isn't dangerous?"

"No. Because the chance of this escaped patient making his way to Pirate's Cove, let alone Captain's Seat, is about one in a million."

"Why was this guy locked up?"

"Edwin Dolph was found not guilty—"

"*Not* guilty?"

"—by reason of insanity of murdering his family with an axe."

"With. An. Axe." Ellery swallowed. "He murdered his family? With an axe!"

Jack made a smothered sound that could have been a laugh. "One in a million, remember?"

"Apparently the cops were all over Point Judith looking for Dolph, so *someone* thinks he's coming our way."

"Unless he's got wings, he's going to find the crossing challenging."

"Where there's a will there's a way."

In an obvious attempt to change the subject, Jack asked, "Are you back at Captain's Seat?"

"No. We're at the Crow's Nest. Everybody wanted to see the bookshop. I think we'll grab a late lunch at the Salty Dog and then head out to the house."

"Okay. Be safe."

"With a homicidal maniac on the loose, you know it."

"I was thinking more of the muddy roads, but okay. I'll see you this evening."

"Be careful, Jack."

Jack said reassuringly, "I'm always careful. Have fun with your friends. I love you."

"I love you, too."

Jack clicked off. Ellery sighed.

From the book floor he could hear Nora in full island historian mode. "The most dangerous of the three escaped patients was thirty-year-old Frank Weeden. Due to his violent criminal history, the papers of the day referred to him as a *homicidal maniac.*"

Chelsea's voice carried even more clearly. "They grow on trees around here!"

Nora said tartly, "That was in 1907, so we enjoy a relatively long harvesting period."

"Uh oh," Ellery murmured, and left his office. "Who wants lunch?"

Tosh, already balancing a short stack of books, was browsing the What's New? shelf. Chelsea stood at the counter with Nora and Kingston, his other employee. Flip knelt in the center aisle, playing with Watson. He sent Watson's ball spinning across the open space, and glanced up. "I could eat something."

"Pass." Lenny still seemed to be suffering the effects of the rough ferry crossing. She sat, well, *drooped*, on the library bench near the front windows.

"A little ginger tea will set you right," Nora told her.

Lenny shuddered.

"Witches can't cross water," Tosh pronounced, rather bafflingly. She set the stack of books on the counter for Nora to ring up.

"No, no," Ellery intervened. "On the house."

Tosh frowned. "Is this a bookstore or a library? You have to make money, Ellery."

"I don't need to make money off my friends."

Tosh turned to Nora. Nora said briskly, "All customers welcome here," and began to ring up the books.

Chelsea cut off Ellery's objections. "Ell, guess what? Homicidal maniacs are a regular thing around here."

Judging by Nora's expression, that comment did not sit well. Kingston cleared his throat. "Not a *regular* thing, no."

Ellery said, "Wait. This has happened before?"

"The circumstances were entirely different," Nora said. "Frank Weeden had been committed to Rhode Island Hospital for Mental Diseases after he tried to shoot his cousin for rejecting his marriage proposal."

"Nobody likes rejection," Flip said, er, flippantly.

"He escaped fifteen times over the years."

"F-F-fifteen times!?" That was Ellery.

"Correct. On his final attempt, he shot and murdered the head of the institution, who he blamed for his being denied parole again."

"With good reason, I'd say."

"Yes, there's little doubt Weeden was a very dangerous individual." Nora delicately plucked Tosh's credit card from her hand.

Ellery asked, "Did he try to escape to the island?"

"No. There's no record of his ever visiting the island at all."

Kingston said, "Even in June, when Weeden broke out, it would have been very foolish to try to hide out here. In November, it would be madness."

Nora handed Tosh her bag of books. They smiled at each other in a silent understanding that Ellery couldn't help feeling was somehow directed at him.

"There are more vacation homes these days. And more empty vacation homes in November," he pointed out.

Nora and Kingston exchanged looks. "True," Nora admitted. "But it would also be much more difficult to reach the island undetected."

"That's settled. We're all doomed." Flip was joking, of course.

Chelsea drawled, "Not Ellery. He's the Final Boy."

The others laughed. Kingston looked puzzled.

"A trope in horror—usually slasher—films," Nora said out of the corner of her mouth. "The Final Girl manages to escape the dreadful fate of her friends or family in order to confront and defeat the evil entity in a final showdown."

"Ah. Horror." Kingston didn't go so far as to grimace, but he was strictly a crime, mystery, and suspense aficionado.

To Watson's great disappointment, Flip gave the ball one final spin, and rose. "Critics labeled Ellery the Final Boy after the fourth *Happy Halloween! You're Dead* film."

Ellery groaned. "Can we not?"

His heartless friends merely chortled at his discomfort.

"Do you know anything about the Dolph case, Nora?" Ellery asked.

"Not really. No."

"Not *really*? So, you know *something.*"

Nora and Kingston had developed a habit of locking eyes when one of them was trying to recall some obscure factoid of island history. Like two computers interfacing.

Following a second or two of visual API, Nora said, "I don't believe there have been Dolphs on this island since the 1930s."

Ellery did a doubletake. "There *is* an island connection."

"Now that's a bit of a stretch." Given that Nora was the queen of drawing conclusions well beyond the reach of ordinary logic or normal reason, her scoffing seemed a little unfair.

Kingston mused, "There's the legend of the Dourdos Aquamarine."

"Sadly, there's little reason to believe it's anything more than legend."

"Since when does anyone in this place dismiss legends?" Ellery demanded.

"Since we have more important things to deal with." Nora ducked behind the sales desk and rose with a square, flat cardboard box, which she handed to Ellery. "These are yours. To do with as you wish."

"These are my what?"

"Your complimentary copies of next year's Gentlemen of Note calendars."

"*Oh.*" Ellery threw a nervous look at his friends and tried to hand the box back to Nora. "Maybe we should keep them here. We can sell them for the Town Council."

Tosh and Chelsea exchanged glances. Chelsea grinned broadly, evilly.

"Gentlemen of Note calendars?" Tosh asked. "Is Ellery a Gentleman of Note?"

Kingston said diplomatically, "We like to think so."

"Certainly!" Nora resisted Ellery's efforts to hand the box off to her. "We already have a box to sell at the Crow's Nest, dearie. These are for your personal use."

"But I don't use wall calendars."

Nora shoved the box firmly back into his arms. "Then this is the perfect opportunity to start. Besides, I'm sure your friends would all *love* a calendar."

Tosh, never one to miss her cue, responded, "*I* would love a calendar. I'll even pay for one."

"It's for a very good cause," Nora assured her.

"What's the cause?" Chelsea asked.

"The Widows and Orphans fund."

"Isn't that supposed to be covered by Social Security or something?"

Nora, mistress of the art of the side eye, offered her profile in answer.

"Is Ellery nekkid?" Flip reached for the box.

Ellery clutched the box to his chest. "No! I'm sure as hell not."

That seemed to crack his friends up all over again.

"No, no," Nora assured them. "It's not that kind of calendar."

"It's *kind* of that kind of calendar," Ellery retorted.

"Nora, we're sold. Break open your stash," Tosh ordered.

And Nora, revealed in all her traitorous colors, did that very thing; used her trusty utility knife to slash open a second square, flat box. She began to hand out calendars and Ellery's friends began to shell out dollars.

"It's for a good cause, my boy," Kingston assured him with a kindly pat on the back.

"That's what they want you to believe, Kingston."

Kingston chuckled.

When the calendars had been purchased, Ellery snapped Watson's leash to his harness and shepherded his flock toward the front door. The wind nearly blew the door shut again.

"We'll see you Saturday night," Nora called. "Can we bring anything?"

"Nope," Ellery replied. "Greta's Gourmandery is handling all the food and Dylan's volunteered to play bartender."

That was a major concession on Dylan's part, given that he'd barely spoken a word to Jack since September. Ellery was hoping that the combination of good food, good company, and enough alcohol might result in, at the least, détente between two of his favorite people.

He held the door against the wind as his friends filed out. Book pages rustled noisily. The framed paintings of pirate ships rocked back and forth on the wall, as if the galleons were truly on the windswept ocean. Ellery raised his hand in farewell.

A hard gust slammed the door, cutting off Nora's cheery, "See you Satur—!"

CHAPTER THREE

"**I** guess we could have picked a time of year with better weather," Chelsea was saying.

An hour after leaving the Crow's Nest, Ellery and his friends were cozily settled in front of the giant fireplace at the Salty Dog. The pub was nearly empty on that damp and chilly November afternoon, which was one reason Watson was allowed to curl up beneath their table, head resting on Ellery's boot. They were just finishing their lunches and a second round of drinks; everyone seemed to be pleasantly tired and very relaxed.

"We had to be invited," Tosh pointed out.

"It's not that I didn't want company," Ellery protested. "The house wasn't in any kind of shape for guests. It was barely livable. The roof was disintegrating. Windows were falling out of their frames. The plumbing was...alarming."

Flip said, "I believe it, going by those first photos you sent."

"Plus, you had all those murders to solve," Lenny teased.

Ellery smiled weakly. "Not really."

"And Brandon, of all people. That was just crazy."

Yes, that had been pretty crazy. For a lot of reasons.

Chelsea said to Flip, "I don't know why you say *of all people*, because if anybody was going to wind up getting murdered, it was Brandon."

Flip frowned. "Kind of harsh, Chels, don't you think?"

"No. I don't. You know the kind of thing he wrote. Pure psycho bait."

"Since when are you a literary critic?" Flip's smile was teasing, but Chelsea looked unamused.

A sudden gust of wind seemed to shake the old building. No one spoke for a moment, which was just as well. This was one conversation Ellery didn't want to have. But then again, Brandon had been at Tisch with them. It was inevitable someone would bring up the subject of his death.

"Is Belle really going to marry an English peer?" Ellery tried to direct the conversation to safer waters.

At the same moment, Chelsea said, "Are there really secret passages in your house?"

"Ellery doesn't want us to know about his secret passages," Lenny joked.

"I'm the one who *told* you about my secret passages. Anyway, secret passages aren't that much of a secret on this island. All the old buildings seem to have them. I'm happy to show you mine."

Flip wiggled his eyebrows but made no comment. Ellery and Flip had dated a couple of times—that was before Ellery met Brandon—but the relationship had never gone anywhere. Probably because Flip was a very decent guy and, until Jack, Ellery had always, infallibly, migrated toward jerks.

Tosh said, "In answer to your question, yes. Belle says she's going to marry Viscount Hate."

"It's pronounced Hat," Chelsea corrected her.

"Is it?"

Ellery said, "That's so crazy. I really thought she and Oscar were going to wind up getting hitched."

"Belle and Oscar?" Tosh seemed startled. "That was over ages ago."

"I know, but they seemed... Well, I guess I don't know."

"No. That was over *ages* ago," Tosh said firmly.

Ellery sensed he was wandering into perilous territory and groped for a less controversial topic of gossip. "How's Freddie doing? I heard he landed the role of Detective Bolton on *LAPD Blues*?"

"Yep. Freddie's crushin' it," Flip said ruefully.

That was the truth. Freddie wasn't the most talented of their group—Flip was a far better actor—but Freddie had arguably had the most successful career. Partly because he had the kind of studly, blond good looks that worked equally well for bad guys *and* good guys.

"He's going to stay in L.A. permanently?"

Tosh said, "I think so."

Chelsea gave her an unreadable look.

That was a relationship that had always puzzled Ellery. Not Freddie and Tosh—well, that too—but Chelsea and Tosh. They had roomed together through most of college and even after, once Tosh and Freddie split up. They had never seemed to have much in common, beyond their theatrical ambitions. Now that Tosh worked as director of special events for the Roundelay Theater Group, they might not even have that. But they'd always seemed tight.

Tosh swallowed a mouthful of grog. "It's funny. This place feels so...familiar. I can't think what it reminds me of." Her blue gaze rested on the diamond-paned windows with their blurry view of the rainy street outside and the weathered Georgian style buildings.

Lenny said, "You mean familiar in a déjà vu way?" Revived by food and drink, Lenny was starting to look more like her usual self. That was not to say there was color in her cheeks—there was never color in her cheeks—but she no longer looked ready to swoon into the remnants of her mac and cheese casserole.

"Not exactly. It's like a play. Cute village full of quirky people who can't keep their noses out of each other's business."

Chelsea's, "Maybe. But I was thinking *Murder, She Wrote*," got a round of chuckles.

"Or *Midsomer Murders*?" Flip suggested.

"No. Ellery can't do accents."

Case in point. Ellery's "*Oi!*" sounded more Brooklyn than British.

Watson, who had heard all the jokes about his village before, groaned from beneath the table.

"Whatever. It's pretty cozy for the murder capital of the Eastern seaboard." Tosh asked, "How *did* you end up getting involved in all those murders, Ellery?"

"Seriously," Chelsea said. "It's not like you were a big fan of crime films."

"I couldn't even get you to go see *Girl with the Dragon Tattoo*." Flip finished his grog. "And now you're...what? A P.I.?"

Ellery choked on his drink. "*What?* No way! No. I don't know. I just...stumble into things." He added, "Don't say *PI* in front of Jack."

The others laughed, which was not reassuring.

"He's way too modest," Tom Tulley arrived with a third round of drinks. "How's the food?"

Everyone lied and assured Tom the food was the best ever.

"You know, it's supposed to snow on Saturday," Tom told Ellery.

"That's what Nora said."

"It's what the National Weather Service says."

"It won't snow a lot, will it?" Tosh asked uneasily. "We're not going to get snowed in or anything?"

Tom laughed heartily. "Nah. Not this time of year. Anything else I can get you folks?"

"The check," Ellery said. "We should get going before the rain gets any worse."

Tom departed and Ellery finished his drink. The others drank and chatted about the rain and the weather and whether they had brought the right clothes for the weekend. Happily, they seemed to have forgotten about the possible homicidal maniac on the loose.

It was both comforting and startling how easily they all slipped into familiar patterns and behaviors, right down to teasing each other about the same old things in the same old ways. But then the past was their common denominator. Maybe this meal had been more about reestablishing old alliances before they embarked on catching up with where they were in their lives now?

"It's just...really hard to picture you here, Ell," Chelsea said suddenly. "You loved New York so much."

Ellery snapped out of his preoccupation. "I did. I do. But I felt like I was out of options in New York."

"How can anyone be out of options in New York?"

Ellery shrugged.

"I can see Ellery here," Tosh said. "I *do* see Ellery here."

"I take that as a compliment."

It wasn't necessarily meant as a compliment. He knew that. He knew his friends still thought he'd retreated from his old life—in their view, *reality*—after his career flatlined and he'd broken up with Todd. And in the beginning that had been at least partly true.

Not anymore. Not at all.

But he didn't expect his old crew to see that. Not yet. Hopefully, by the end of the weekend, they'd understand.

Tom returned with the check, which Flip snatched from Ellery's hand.

"We've got this."

The inevitable wrangle ensued, which Ellery lost, then everyone gulped down the last of their drinks, shrugged into their coats and scarves, and headed for the door.

"See you Saturday!" Tom called.

For some reason it seemed a lot more difficult piling into the VW the third time than it had the first and second.

But at last, damp and breathless, Lenny, Tosh, and Chelsea were shoehorned into the backseat. Ellery handed Watson to Tosh for safekeeping. Flip buckled up in the passenger seat.

"What's the world record for cramming people into a Volkswagen?" Chelsea gasped as Lenny tried to shift position. "*Ooof!*"

"Sorry," Lenny muttered.

"It's okay. They say you don't really need your appendix."

Watson began to whine.

Tosh said, "This reminds me of Freddie's first car. Minus the puppy."

"The Datsun 280ZX?" Flip turned in his seat to grin at Chelsea. "The one Chelsea almost wrecked."

"I did not! At least I always returned it with a full tank. Unlike the rest of you freeloaders."

"Ouch."

"Don't look at me. I don't drive," Lenny said.

"Right," Tosh said. "And when we'd go anywhere together, Ellery had to curl up in the trunk."

"It was a hatchback," Ellery objected. "I didn't travel in the trunk!"

Lenny said, "I'm still not sure why the tallest person was the one who had to fold up in the cargo area like a Gumby."

There was a moment of silence.

"*Now* she mentions it," Ellery said.

The fact that they all found that hysterical was probably a testament to Tom Tulley's tendency toward a heavy pour.

Ellery, fortunately for all, had stuck to one beer. He started the VW. Watson tried to make a break for the front seat, but was restrained by three pairs of hands. All the sweet words and petting could not distract from the wrongs being done him. He began to yip with increasing vehemence, his protests sounding even louder than usual in the confined space.

As they hit the cobbled streets of Pirate's Cove, Watson reached air raid siren amplification.

Ar-ar-oooooo! Ar-ar-arooooo! AR-AR—

"Yikes," Tosh said. "Home, James. And don't spare the horses!"

CHAPTER FOUR

They were still arguing over Ellery's record for parking tickets acquired in one year when Captain's Seat came into view.

"Holy…" Flip's voice gave out. "Is that *it*?"

There was an instant and respectful silence at the rainswept vision of 18th Century architectural absurdity. Lights blazed from the many windows, and the blue-black granite exterior seemed to glow against the stormy skies. Even Watson, who had been relentless in his petition for an upgrade to first class, seemed to pause for breath.

Ellery nodded. "Home, sweet home."

"*Wow.*" That was Tosh. "That is…"

"Totally extra," Ellery said. "I know."

Chelsea said, "It's *three* stories?"

"I mean, not really. The third story is mostly just attic and weird little rooms that I think were used as servants' quarters. It's not even heated."

"Is it haunted?" Lenny asked. "Because it looks haunted."

"Well…"

The others laughed, but Ellery was reserving judgment on that last question. The house had its eccentricities, no doubt.

"You could make a killing renting out that top level," Chelsea was saying. "The crew on the ship over was complaining about how the housing prices over here are totally out of control."

"Real estate's at a premium on the island." Ellery couldn't argue with that. "But other than the wiring, the top level hasn't been renovated at all. I don't even like to go up there. It's pretty creepy." Which was true. But also, he had zero desire to be anyone's landlord. He liked his privacy. And, more important, Jack liked his privacy.

Captain's Seat loomed ever larger in the rain speckled windshield as they drew near.

Chelsea said, "If you were to sell—"

"I would never sell. Captain's Seat has been in my family since the 1700s."

Ellery said it firmly, which was funny given that he'd arrived on Buck Island convinced he would do that very thing. Now, nine months later, he was talking like Belle's viscount.

Watson, who had barely let up on the backseat driving since leaving Pirate's Cove, reached full crescendo as Ellery pulled into the small front courtyard that served as the parking area. His passengers gawped at the fanciful Dutch gables, stained-glass windows, and twin conical-shaped rooftops.

"Be it ever so humble," Flip said.

Ellery glanced back at Tosh, Chelsea, and Lenny. "Should I get a crowbar?"

Chelsea said, "For the love of God. Open the door. For the love of God—"

"It's going to be like opening a can of snakes," Tosh warned. "Open the door and stand clear."

"I can't feel my legs," Lenny moaned.

Ellery and Flip hastily opened their doors and got out. Watson scrambled into the front seat, leaped to the ground, and shook himself indignantly. Flip assisted Chelsea as Ellery shoved his seat forward and helped Tosh out. She was swearing colorfully as she unfolded from the back.

Lenny followed, crawling out on her hands and knees.

Watson ran a couple of laps around the VW, barking manically, and raced off to the back of the house.

"I feel you, dog," Lenny called after him.

Chelsea said, "Oh, my GOD. I'm *walking* back to the ferry." The others looked at her as though she were insane. "No, not *now*. When it's time to leave!"

"Why are we talking about leaving when we just got here?" Flip asked.

"I may never lie flat again," Tosh told Ellery. "But I'm willing to try."

"Right." Ellery called, "This way, guys." He led the way across the sparkling wet white gravel, past the dripping rose bushes, to find a small mountain of luggage neatly stacked on the slick steps in front of the door.

Ezra Christmas had been and gone in his venerable taxi.

"Here, let's just make some room." Ellery worked his way around the luggage, unlocked the heavy front door, and pushed it open as the others reclaimed their suitcases and bags.

Watery light flooded from the overhead windows, moodily illuminating the gleaming patchwork of ship's timber flooring and old paintings on the white oak panels, and the banisters built to look like the row of cannons on the broadside of a warship.

For the first time in months, the "great hall" was empty of drop cloths, saw horses, ladders, paint cans, and various scattered tools. For the first time in months, Ellery could see the house as it had been meant to be seen.

There was a chorus of gasps from behind him.

"*Very* cool," Lenny said, staring at the arched segmental windows reminiscent of those on a pirate galleon. "Who's your decorator? Captain Hook?"

Ellery's laugh was a little shaky because, crazy as it was, he was actually moved at how beautiful the house was—and how much it felt like home. Not really logical, given that Captain's Seat had in fact been his home for the last eight months, but somehow this weird moment with the rain pattering down and his guests complaining about the drive as they dragged their luggage inside, and the faint smell of paint still lingering in the air, felt like his official home-coming.

"Seriously, it's *beautiful*, Ell," Tosh exclaimed.

"It really is." Flip squeezed Ellery's shoulder. "Congratulations."

Ellery said, "It's been a journey. You should have seen it the afternoon I arrived. Anyway, the bedrooms are on the second floor. If you guys want to get settled, I can give you the grand tour before dinner."

"Lead on, Macduff." Flip shouldered his knapsack.

Chelsea said, "You know it's *Lay on,* Macduff, right?"

Flip sighed. "I know we're not performing the play, Chelse. *That* I'm sure of."

"*Aww*. They need their naps," Lenny murmured.

"Here we go, here we go!" Ellery borrowed a leaf from Kingston's Saturday Storytime repertoire. He didn't actually clap his hands, but it went through his mind. "Follow me!" He started up the staircase. "Like I mentioned in my email, there are five bedrooms. Each bedroom shares a bath with the bedroom next door..."

"We've worked it out, don't worry," Tosh told him. "Belle and I are together. Lenny and Flip are bunkies. Chelsea needs her own room, so I guess Freddie and Oscar can figure it out when they get here."

Ellery opened his mouth and closed it. That would not have been his stage blocking, but he wasn't about to second guess anybody on where they chose to lay their heads and other body parts.

Flip remarked, "I wouldn't want to miss a step in the dark on these stairs."

The staircase was treacherous, no lie. Jack had stepped on one of Watson's squeaky toys the previous week, and nearly lost his balance.

However, his guests and their luggage reached the second-floor landing out of breath but without incident.

"Okay, well, here we are—" Ellery opened the first and largest bedroom door. "Tosh, this is you and Belle. Flip and Lenny are on the other side, sharing a bath with you. Chelsea, you're on the end. The bathroom is—"

Chelsea interrupted, "*Oh*! Could I maybe switch with Oscar? I get nervous in old houses. I'd rather not be way out on the end. Or even Freddie. I don't care. I just, you know."

It was pretty much the worst performance of her life, and the look Tosh and Lenny shared indicated the reviews would not be kind.

"Uh, sure," Ellery said. "Right this way."

As the others vanished into their rooms, Ellery turned and led the way down the hall in the opposite direction.

Chelsea was asking, "I guess it gets pretty cold here at night?"

"It does," Ellery admitted. "But the bedrooms all have fireplaces—which reminds me. I need to chop more wood. I wasn't expecting snow."

"You mean there's no heat?"

"No, there's central heating. It's just sort of at will."

"Whose will?"

"The house's?" Ellery opened the door across from the master bedroom. "How about this room? Will this do?"

Chelsea didn't bother to glance inside the room. "Perfect!" She stepped inside the room. "I'll be down to grab the rest of my bags in a few." She smiled sweetly and shut the door in Ellery's face.

Ellery did not actually chop his own firewood. He had wood delivered, like most of the island's inhabitants. He did, however, chop his own kindling, and after delivering Chelsea's luggage to her door, he spent a very damp forty minutes making sure his guests would have everything they needed to warm their bedrooms before turning in for the night.

With the arbitrariness of island weather, the rain finally let up as he was finishing. The damp air was sweet and cold. He carried the kindling into the house, asked Watson if he wanted to go for a quick walk—a rhetorical question if there ever was one—and headed out again.

As they started down the drive, he spotted another hooded figure up ahead. Watson began to bark. Ellery whistled sharply. The figure stopped, turned, and waved. Ellery relaxed. Flip.

Who had he thought it was? Axe murderer Edwin Dolph?

"I thought I'd stretch my legs." Flip's breath hung in the air as he reached Ellery and Watson.

Watson, already losing interest in any visitor who wasn't Jack, darted off across the sodden meadow.

Ellery smiled. "We're just walking down to the beach."

"You want some company?"

"Sure!"

In accord, they started across the meadow, sticking to the path, unlike Watson who could be seen bounding his way over—and through—goldenrod, fading bayberry, wild field roses, and the scarlet flashes of bittersweet.

"It really is beautiful," Flip acknowledged.

"It grows on you."

"Mm."

The rain pattered down around them, whispering on the hoods of their parkas. Their boots thudded on the sodden trail.

Yards ahead, Watson did his best to keep them abreast of current events.

Arf! Arf! Arf!

Ellery glanced at Flip's unusually solemn profile.

Flip had brown hair, green eyes, a pointy chin, and a wide, mobile mouth that curved easily and frequently into a genuinely beautiful smile. He was not classically handsome, not like Freddie, but he had the kind of attractiveness that did not fade with time.

He stared ahead at the now flea-sized Watson "It doesn't feel cold enough for snow."

"It's pretty cold."

Flip had never been one for long walks in the rain, so Ellery was pretty sure he was trying to work himself up to broach something he didn't want to broach. There was only one such topic Ellery could think of, and he wanted to hear it as little as Flip wanted to say it.

They walked in an increasingly awkward silence for another minute or two and then Flip said, "I saw Todd on Tuesday."

Just as Ellery had expected. Well, forewarned was fore-armed.

"Yeah?" Ellery did not care, did not want to hear it.

"It's all over with him and Jerry."

Ellery said nothing.

"I guess it's been over for months."

"What a surprise." Ellery couldn't help the tinge of bitterness that crept into his voice. "And they were so perfect for each other, too."

Flip made a sound of acknowledgement. "You know where I stand."

Presumably. Flip had known Ellery a lot longer than he'd known Todd or Jerry. But if Flip was bringing this up now, it was with purpose and Ellery braced himself.

"He's got a lot of regrets."

"I would hope so." Ellery glanced at Flip. Flip's expression was troubled. "I trusted them. I would hope they're both regretful."

"I can't speak for Jerry, but Todd was strongly hinting that he'd like me to try to...I don't know. Test the waters."

Ellery threw him a look of disbelief. "*Test the waters*? What, are we back at Tisch? The water is ice cold. The water is at freezing point and Todd would be dead in fifteen minutes if he tried jumping in."

Flip said quickly, awkwardly, "I hear you."

"Seriously, if Todd has something to say to me, he should man up and say it to *me*."

"I know. I know, I told him that." After a moment, Flip asked, "*Would* you want to hear from him?"

"No." Ellery was definite.

"Because of Jack?"

"Because of *Todd*." Ellery added, "But also because of Jack, yeah. I *love* Jack." In fact, he loved Jack more than

Todd, Brandon, and every other guy he'd ever dated, combined.

Flip considered that, glanced at Ellery, and smiled tentatively. "I'm looking forward to meeting Jack."

Ellery forced himself to smile in answer. "Me, too. I really want him to meet all of you."

"I hope you don't—aren't—"

"You mean well. I know that."

"Yeowch."

Ellery managed a short laugh, but honestly? Flip should have known better.

By then they had reached the steep hillside trail leading down to the beach. Watson scampered down, but Ellery stopped Flip, with a hand on his arm. "It's not safe when it's been raining." He spoke from painful experience.

From their vantage point, they gazed down at churning white water. The sea was running high; the tide sweeping up the empty beach in long rollers. The fuzzy white sun turned the crescent of sand stretching north eerily, unnaturally bright. Watson raced along the water's edge, chasing the waves away, then nearly somersaulting in retreat when the water rushed back.

Flip chuckled, watching him.

"He never gets tired of that game. Well, of *any* game," Ellery commented.

Eventually, Ellery whistled for Watson, who came charging up the hillside, not bothering with the trail at all. The three of them started back to the house.

Flip asked, "Do you think you'd be staying on the island if Jack wasn't part of the deal?"

Ellery didn't have to think about it. "Yes. My decision to stay was made when Jack and I were just friends."

"You don't miss New York?"

"Sometimes. But it's not like I can't visit New York if I want to."

"True."

Ellery studied Flip quizzically.

"I miss you," Flip admitted. "I know you're only about five hours away—"

"Less than that, if you grab a flight."

"But you used to be half an hour away."

Also true. But even when Ellery and Flip had lived half an hour away from each other, they'd gone weeks, sometimes months without getting together. Ellery didn't say that, though. He looped his arm around Flip's shoulders and gave him a quick hug.

"I know. I miss you, too. I miss all of you. Hopefully, this is the first of many regular visits."

"I hope so." Flip didn't sound entirely convinced.

CHAPTER FIVE

Ellery was in the kitchen checking on the roast when Tosh came downstairs carrying a square blue box.

"Something smells delicious," she said.

"Country chuck roast with veg, mashed potatoes, and mushroom gravy."

"Oh my gosh. That sounds like heaven. I can't believe I'm already hungry again. It must be the salt air." She set the box on the table. "What can I do to help?"

"There's a bottle of wine on the dining room table if you want to open it."

Tosh briefly disappeared, reappeared with a bottle of merlot, and went straight to the counter drawer to the left of the sink. She pulled out the wing corkscrew, held it up, and grinned. "Some things never change."

Ellery pretend-frowned. "Are you saying I'm predictable?"

"In all the best possible ways."

He considered, conceded, but said, "*Some* things change."

Maybe Tosh followed his thoughts. As she opened the wine, she said, "I saw you and Flip walking back to the house. Did he tell you about Todd?"

"Yep."

Tosh shook her head. "I told him to butt out. But he insisted you should know."

Ellery couldn't help an acerbic, "Know what? That Jerry and Todd wouldn't last? I already knew that." He gave a short laugh and changed the subject. "Where's everybody else?"

"Lenny's still lying down, I think. The trip over really took it out of her. It sounded like Flip was in the shower. Chelsea is… doing whatever."

Ellery was momentarily distracted. "I can't get over the change in Chelsea."

"Yep. It's quite the transformation." Tosh's tone was dry, which was interesting. If anyone knew Chelsea, it was Tosh.

"What do you think sparked it? She was always so adamantly…*au naturale*."

"*Toujours l'amour, archie*." That was one of Tosh's catch phrases from back in the day. It was a quote from a book called the *The Best of Archy and Mehitabel*, which no one but Tosh had read.

"Seriously? You think she's in love?"

"With Hollywood stardom. Yes."

"*Chelsea?* She always scorned the idea of Tinseltown."

"Did she, though?" Again, that certain dryness in Tosh's tone. "Well, she doesn't scorn the idea of working steadily. Or getting paid a living wage. Plus, Freddie's *so* pro Hollywood, so pro West Coast." Tosh got a couple of wine glasses out of the cupboard and poured the merlot.

"He's probably lonely out there."

"*Freddie?* I seriously doubt Freddie's pining for company.*"

If it was true about past being prologue, then she was probably right.

Ellery closed the oven, admitted, "I haven't really talked to Freddie in a while."

"Well, you kind of fell off the grid, Ell. Plus, it's not like *you* need Freddie's help."

No. It wasn't. Still.

"To be honest, I'm not sure Chelsea would tell me if there *was* someone." Tosh handed a glass of wine to Ellery.

"Really?"

"Cheers."

"Cheers." They clinked glasses.

"We don't talk like we used to," Tosh admitted. She met Ellery's gaze. "No big drama. Our lives, our careers, are going in different directions now."

That was the challenge for friendships formed in college. Tosh and Chelsea had always been the odd couple in their little circle, but they had seemed genuinely close. Ellery changed the subject. "What's in the box?"

Tosh brightened. "Photos. Our misspent youth in living color."

"Uh oh."

Tosh started to reply, but they were interrupted by the appearance of Watson, who trotted into the kitchen proudly dragging a long burnt-orange wool scarf behind him.

Ellery gasped and jumped to rescue the scarf. Watson, naturally, assumed they were playing an impromptu but delightful game of tug-o-war. He growled ferociously, chomped down on the scarf, and dug his little heels in.

"No, Watson," Ellery said severely.

Watson growled again, wagged his tail, pulled harder on his half of the scarf.

"Watson, *drop it.*"

That was a tone Watson had rarely heard, and he dropped the scarf at once. His wounded expression was disconcertingly humanlike.

Ellery snatched the scarf up, scanning it for—and finding—tiny toothmarks. He groaned. "Cashmere."

"Cashmere blend," Tosh said. "It's Chelsea's."

Ellery glanced up in surprise. "Meow."

Tosh blushed, protested, "No. It's just…it's Chelsea's scarf."

Ellery gazed sternly down at his woebegone little pal. "Thanks a lot, Jaws."

But it seemed Watson heard something in Ellery's tone, because his ears perked and he gave a tentative wag of his tail.

"Yeah, well, it's coming out of your allowance." Ellery folded up the scarf and laid it on the counter.

"Awww. My gosh, he's cute."

"Remember that when he's chewing on your boots."

"No, he wouldn't. Look at that sweet little face." Tosh scooped up Watson and kissed his sweet little face. Watson bore up manfully—or pupfully—under these attentions.

"Something sure smells terrific!" Flip appeared in the doorway, followed by Lenny, who said, "We're going to have to time our showers. I'm pretty sure Chelsea ran out of hot water. We could hear her screaming from down the hall. She sounded like she was being murdered."

Flip concurred. "The hot water ran out while I was showering."

Tosh said, "We didn't hear a thing downstairs."

"You can hear the wind." Lenny shivered. "It's whispering from every corner of the house. It's so dark and desolate out here. How do you stand it, Ellery?"

He shrugged. "You get used to it."

"*Do* you?"

Ellery chuckled. "Of course."

"You're not nervous at all? It's as dark as night outside. The wind sounds like the sea is rushing the house."

In fairness, he'd been a little jumpy those first couple of months. The house—especially back then—had been more than a little spooky. Ellery said bracingly, "Yeah, but it's not."

"Not *yet*."

Flip laughed at Lenny.

"There's wine." Ever the pragmatist, Tosh held up the wine bottle.

"Thank *God*," Lenny said.

Flip sat down at the table, lifting the lid off the large blue box. "Whoa. Tosh, are these your photos from Tisch?"

Tosh, getting more wine glasses out of the cupboard, glanced over her shoulder. "Hm? Yes! I was thinking it'd be fun to go through them together."

"That's a great idea. I don't have any pics from back then. In fact, I don't have a lot of photos from now. I never think of taking them," Flip said.

"Same." Lenny clicked her wine glass against Tosh's. "Cheers."

"Oh! *Wait*," Tosh exclaimed. "We have to toast!"

"Didn't I just—"

"No, *formally* toast."

Ellery tossed his oven mitt aside and picked up his glass. "What are we *formally* toasting to?"

"Flip, you're good at this part," Tosh said.

Flip obediently rose, held up his glass and announced, "To old friends and new memories."

They all smiled at each other.

"That's a nice one." Ellery clinked his glass against Tosh's and Lenny's. As he and Flip clicked rims, he teased, "Do you have a list of toasts memorized for every occasion?"

Flip grinned. "I do. Yeah."

"How about for St. Paddy's?" Tosh challenged.

In an alarmingly broad Irish accent, Flip said solemnly, "Over me nose, and down it goes."

Lenny choked on her wine. The others laughed.

Tosh said to Ellery, "Fair warning, we're probably going to drink you out of house and home."

"You can try. I prepared for the onslaught."

"That's our boy." Lenny patted his shoulder. Her gaze moved past him; her eyes widened. "*Uhhhhh*... Is that Chelsea's scarf?"

Ellery glanced over in time to see Watson tugging at the end of Chelsea's scarf, which hung enticingly over the edge of the counter. He gasped and lunged for the scarf.

"Watson, NO."

Watson's ears flattened and he looked at the others like, *do you hear how he speaks to me?*

"Oops, that was my fault." Tosh topped up Ellery's wine glass. "I moved the scarf."

"Aww. You hurt his feelings," Flip patted his thighs. "Come here, little pal."

Watson leaped onto Flip's lap and gave Ellery a pointed look. Ellery made an amused sound, shook his head, "Don't encourage him."

"You talking to him or me?"

"Oh my gosh, we didn't wait for Chelsea!" Tosh's guilt gave way to sudden unease. "Hey, where *is* she, anyway?"

There was a startled moment of silence.

"Did someone take my name in vain?" Chelsea called from the hallway.

Everyone relaxed, breathed, what seemed to Ellery, a small collective sigh of relief.

"What are you doing lurking in the hallway?" Lenny called.

"I wasn't *lurking*." Chelsea sounded ever so slightly irritated as she joined them.

Was it his imagination or, now that it was dark outside, was everyone maybe a wee bit on edge?

"Then your shadow was," Lenny retorted.

Chelsea made a face at Lenny, but didn't bite.

Ellery and Tosh exchanged glances.

In fairness, they'd been traveling most of the day. Everyone was tired and maybe his friends really did find the house spooky. Nor were they kids anymore. It had been a long time since they'd been together like this, and they weren't the same people now. Things that had been fall-down-laughing funny in college—like taking a nap and waking up plastic-wrapped to a sofa—would probably not go over quite as well now.

As adults, they simply might not have as much in common. It was a sad thought, but that was the truth.

Or perhaps their experience in Point Judith had genuinely rattled them. The idea that a murderous maniac could possibly be skulking around the island was a *little* unsettling, though from a commonsense perspective—from Jack's perspective—it was pretty improbable.

Chelsea took a sip from her wine glass and her micro-bladed eyebrows shot up. "Nice!"

Ellery sighed. "Yes, I finally outgrew Blue Nun."

"Oh my God, you and your Blue Nun." Chelsea shook her head.

"That's what *she* said," Flip joked and, probably due to the previous glasses of not-Blue- Nun, it got a *way* bigger laugh than it deserved. From everyone but Chelsea who did not so much as crack a smile.

Ellery studied her with renewed curiosity.

Chelsea had changed into navy leggings and a baby-blue oversized Fair Isle sweater that looked very similar to the black leggings and oatmeal-and-black oversized Fair Isle sweater Tosh wore. Which Ellery probably wouldn't have noticed—he didn't pay a lot of attention to women's fash-ion—if he hadn't caught Tosh's expression once she got a clear view of Chelsea.

It was a fleeting reaction—Tosh recovered instantly— but just for a second she looked shocked and a little hurt.

But Chelsea really had undergone an amazing makeover. Her hair, her makeup... The change was dramatic but it was also a little baffling. True, if she'd set her sights on Hol-lywood, well, the movie business most certainly favored young, attractive actors over young maybe-not-so attractive actors. That was the nature of the business.

But Tosh knew all that, and her reaction—though quick-ly covered—had been revealing. Hopefully they were not about to have a *Single White Female* moment in their little clique? It seemed like if that had been going to happen, it would have been during their formative college years.

"There was no hot water. *None.*" Chelsea was saying. "I'm pretty sure I have hypothermia."

Ellery winced. The plumbing had a tendency to blast out Arctic-cold water at inopportune times. "Sorry. A new hot water tank is on the list."

Tosh gave Chelsea an exasperated look. "Ellery, what can we do to help?"

Ellery considered. "Would someone want to peel potatoes?"

Flip raised his hand. "Manual labor. That's me."

Tosh said, "You need me to chop veggies?"

"Thanks. That would help." It had been a very long time since he'd cooked for a crowd.

"I'll take over the mashed potatoes when Flip's finished peeling," Lenny took possession of Watson, who was basking in this abundance of attention.

"Great. The potatoes are in the larder. And if someone—"

Chelsea said quickly, "I'll find some music and open another bottle of wine, shall I?"

Tosh made a sound, not quite of derision, and now it was Chelsea's turn to look surprised and hurt.

"Uh, yeah, that would be great."

Yep, there were new, new to him anyway, tensions in their small circle. But maybe a good meal, good wine, and good company would patch some of the fraying of those old school ties.

And it did feel just like old times as everyone set about their appointed tasks in helping to prepare the meal.

So much so, that when Lenny observed, "Is anyone else getting *The Big Chill* meets *I Married an Axe Murderer* vibe?" they all laughed.

"I really don't think we have anything to worry about," Ellery said.

"Oh my God," Flip protested. "Don't *say* that!"

"Thanks a lot. You've just sealed our fate!" Lenny told Ellery.

Tosh, swaying to "In the End" as she chopped veggies, winked at Ellery.

Ellery was turning down the heat on the gravy, when Chelsea, sitting at the table with Flip, said suddenly, "Tosh, are those your photos from Tisch?"

Tosh, chopping at Godspeed, glanced over her shoulder. "Not just school photos, but yes."

Chelsea drew the large box over and removed the lid. She lifted out a stack of pictures.

"Oh, wow. I haven't seen these in years." She began to slowly shuffle through the stack, raising her brows now and then, before shuffling on.

Flip, scrolling through his phone, said, "Okay, I just got a text from Oscar. He says he and Freddie think they'll be docking around 10:00 tomorrow morning, depending on the weather. Belle hasn't confirmed yet."

"No problem." Ellery lifted the pot of boiling potatoes and moved to the sink, carefully pouring the potatoes and steaming water into a large colander. His cell rang. He set the pot aside, pulled out his phone. Jack's photo flashed up. Ellery sighed. He pressed the green button.

Already resigned, he said, "You're not going to make dinner, are you?"

Jack's pleasantly deep voice was apologetic. "I'm sorry. You know I wanted to be there."

"I do know, yep. No worries. Is everything okay there?"

"Everything's fine," Jack said firmly.

Too firmly.

An impression confirmed, when Ellery asked, "*Is* it?"

"Yes. That said, do me a favor and don't take your friends for any moonlight strolls."

"Uh... Okay."

"And go ahead and set the security system now."

"Now?"

"Yes."

Ellery took a moment to absorb that before asking carefully, "Are you saying what I think you're saying?"

"Mm-hm." Jack added in a carefully neutral tone, "That's a qualified yes. There's no actual confirmation, but it's looking more like a possibility."

"A possibility? How strong a possibility?"

Jack's tone stayed neutral despite the alarming words, "Maybe more probability than possibility."

"Fantastic."

"I know. But it's not for sure. There's no need to worry your friends."

Ellery rolled his eyes. "Riiight." If Jack imagined for one minute that Ellery was going to withhold from his friends the information that there was even a *chance* a dangerous mental hospital escapee was loose on the island, he was very much mistaken.

"At the same time, there's also no reason not to take extra precautions."

"Got it," Ellery said.

For once Jack failed to read the room. Seemingly under the illusion that he had reassured Ellery that everything was under control, he said, "I still plan on driving out tonight. But it might be late. I definitely won't make dinner."

"Yeah, well. All things considered, I'll be delighted if we see you this weekend at all."

Jack laughed. "No, it's not like that. We're being extra vigilant. That's all."

"Uh huh."

"Don't worry. And don't worry your friends. Everything will be fine. I'll see you later tonight."

"Okay. *Please* be careful."

"Absolutely. And that goes both ways." Someone spoke in the background. Jack said quietly, "Gotta go. I love you. I'll see you later."

"Love you," Ellery said quickly.

The phone on the other end clicked. Ellery sighed, disconnected. When he glanced up, he found the room was silent, his friends staring at him with open alarm.

"Yep," he said. "We're all gonna die."

CHAPTER SIX

"**N**ot all of us," Tosh said. "*You'll* survive."

The others laughed, and Watson, gazing up at them, wagged his tail. Watson was the original party animal.

"That's right, Final Boy," Flip said. "*You'll* be still be around for the closing credits."

"I can't decide if this is meta or just *macabre*." Chelsea made a little face—and Tosh, watching her, made a little face back. Not in agreement. In friendly mockery. Or maybe not-so- friendly mockery. Chelsea looked confused.

Lenny, not hearing whatever Tosh had heard in Chelsea's comment, responded, "Both!" Which got another round of laughs.

Ellery smiled absently. He was rewinding his conversation with Jack, listening for what Jack *hadn't* said. When Jack said he and his team were being extra vigilant, Ellery believed him. But that didn't mean extra vigilance wasn't required. In his view, a dangerous escaped prisoner—with or without a history of axe murders—would seem to indicate a need for hyper-vigilance.

"I think we're going to need a bigger bottle." Tosh held up the half empty wine bottle.

This was met with murmurs of agreement.

"You don't hear me arguing." Ellery picked up the colander of steaming potatoes, dumped them back in their pot, and set the pan on the stovetop. "Lenny, you're up."

"I can't tell you how much I've missed this," Flip said toward the end of what had indeed been a great dinner.

As Ellery had hoped, plenty of good food, good wine, and good company had everyone relaxed and in good spirits.

"Right?" Tosh beamed. "This is so nice. I've missed you guys."

"Same," Ellery said. In fact, he hadn't realized until they were all together how much he'd missed getting together to reminisce over old times, laugh at shared memories and little inside jokes. He had friends in Pirate's Cove. Good friends. But there was something different about friends with whom you shared a long history.

"Oh yeah, that," Flip said. "But I meant Ellery's cooking!"

This, given how much they'd all had to drink, struck everyone as hilarious, and their laughter woke up Watson, who had finally given up trying to wheedle treats and had fallen asleep on Ellery's feet.

"Everything was perfect," Chelsea said, and the others agreed. "The china, the crystal, the silver—"

"The *food*," Lenny put in, and there was more laughter.

"Anybody save room for dessert?"

This was met by groans and "maybe laters," and they set about clearing the table and getting the dishes out of the way—which took no time at all with so many helping hands.

"So, what's it going to be?" Lenny rubbed her hands together as the final long stemmed wine glass slid into the cupboard. "Clue? Charades? Pictionary?"

"We're going to break Ellery's heart if we don't let him destroy us at Scrabble," Flip said.

Which was true, but Ellery said nobly, "How about after dinner drinks and we go through Tosh's photos?"

"I'd love that," Tosh said, and the others agreed, except Chelsea, who said, "Wait. What about our tour of the house?"

"Oh. Whatever you guys want."

Tosh said quickly, "I'm fine with either. A house tour works for me. There's no rush on the photos."

"It's such a beautiful house," Chelsea enthused.

"Yes. Absolutely," Tosh said.

"Well, I'll give you the grand tour," Ellery said. "And we can go from there."

Everyone expressed joy at this turn of events, though Ellery was pretty sure hot drinks by the fireplace and a photographic walk down Memory Lane would have been the preferred choice of everyone but Chelsea. The house got a little chilly this time of the evening. But okay.

He led the way back to the main hall, Watson scampering ahead. Watson was hugely disappointed when he realized they were not going outside, and plopped down in front of the large wooden door with a woebegone expression on his face.

"Later, pal," Ellery promised. "We'll go later."

"Maybe we should go now," Flip objected. "While we're all together."

"Right," Tosh said. "There's safety in numbers."

"I *really* don't think there's any—"

But he was loudly overruled.

Lenny said, "Ellery, you weren't there. You didn't see. Those cops at Point Judith weren't fooling around. They were dead serious about trying to find that guy."

"Which is why I don't want those guys going out there."

"You think you *alone* out there is a better idea?"

"Watson will protect me." He was kidding, of course, but his friends weren't having it.

"Len's right," Flip said. "This guy is an *axe murderer*."

"Well, true, but even if Dolph somehow made it onto the island, he wouldn't have his axe with—" Even as the words left Ellery's mouth, he remembered he'd left the hatchet he'd used to chop kindling in the stump by the woodpile. He swallowed the rest of it with a little gulp.

"There's safety in numbers," Tosh said firmly. "Anyway, you can't expect poor little Watson to hold it forever."

As if following every word of this conversation, poor little Watson wagged his tail hopefully and glanced meaningfully at the door, just in case Ellery *still* wasn't getting the message.

Jack couldn't have been thinking about Watson when he'd ordered Ellery to batten down the hatches, and Flip had a point. A group of people was less likely to be accosted than one lone person with a small dog.

Ellery sighed. "I guess. Okay, you guys will want your jackets. It's cold. I'll grab a flashlight and Watson's leash—*Wait!*"

It was no use. Reverting to type, his former housemates threw open the door bolt and spilled out into the night with cheery assurances that the triangle of porchlight would be all the illumination necessary and anyway how cold could it be for hardened New Yorkers?

Watson led the way, bounding off into the darkness, blithely ignoring the chorus of calls for him to stay close, stop, and come back.

"*Are you flipping kidding me?*" Ellery demanded of the generations of Pages who had come before, and no, for once he most certainly did *not* say *flipping*. He sprinted back to the kitchen, grabbed a high-powered LED flashlight, Watson's leash, and raced after his errant houseguests—who he could hear wandering down the drive loudly whistling and calling for his less-than-faithful canine companion.

"Watson! Watson! Come on, boy! Come on, good doggie! Here, boy!" cried the ever more distant voices of Ellery's houseguests.

And, more faintly, in the distance, "Arf! Arf! Arf!"

Ellery pounded down the road in hot pursuit, the beam of his flashlight bouncing along ahead of him. Fortunately, the half-moon slid out from behind the cloud cover, and the road and surrounding meadow were all bathed in bright silvery light. It didn't take him long to spot the long unsteady shadows of his guests just ahead.

"You guys! Tosh! Flip! *Hey!* Stop. Lenny! Chelsea..."

It was doubtful they could hear him over their own cries to Watson who, predictably, was exercising selective hearing.

Ellery jogged to a halt and put his fingers to his lips, whistling sharply. The sound pierced the night, cutting through the babble up ahead and the faraway barks.

"Here we are!" Tosh yelled.

Flip yelled, "Over here!"

"This way!" Lenny shouted. "Follow the sound of our voices!"

Did they think *Ellery* was lost?

He muttered, "For crying out," and then called, "Guys, *this* way! You need to come back!"

He spun around at the rustle and crack of something large moving through the brush beside the road, and swung the high-powered flashlight in the direction of the sound. The bright white beam spotlighted dried switchgrass and huckleberry bushes stripped bare by the winter winds. As he watched, the bushes stopped moving. Ellery's scalp prickled.

The flashlight beam probed the bulky shadows, but only found deeper shadows.

Nothing moved. He could hear the babble of voices from down the road and the more distant sound of the tide, but the meadow was almost eerily still.

The odds of a stray cow or a hungry deer were a lot higher than Edwin Dolph skulking through the brush. Although cows and deer rarely stayed motionless for long.

The next instant, he heard the jingle of dog tags and turned. The flashlight caught the gleam of Watson's eyes as he raced back down the road to Ellery. Watson circled Ellery a couple of times, as though inviting him to give chase.

"Did you deliberately take them out to lose them?" Ellery demanded.

Watson, tongue lolling in a goofy grin, circled Ellery one more time and tore off back down the road toward home.

If there had been anything hiding in the tall grass and bushes, wouldn't Watson have noticed?

Ellery turned at the sound of approaching footsteps— well, truthfully, it sounded like a slow-moving stampede.

"Whose idea was this?" Chelsea's voice floated through the darkness.

"You want me to answer that?" Ellery called.

This was greeted with guilty laughter.

"Did you see Watson?" Tosh asked, as they reached Ellery. "He came back this way."

"He sure did," Ellery said acerbically.

Flip said hurriedly, "Okay, before you say anything—"

"I don't even know what to say."

Lenny slipped her arm through Ellery's. "Good. It'll be our little secret."

Tosh took his other arm. "Exactly. You don't have to tell Jack. Not until he gets to know us."

"I'm not lying to Jack," Ellery said seriously.

Chelsea, already walking ahead on the way back to the house, threw back, "No sane person would ask *you* to lie. But you don't have to rush to tell him what a bad influence we are."

"Let him find out for himself," Tosh put in. "Hopefully, he won't even notice."

"You don't want to place undue influence on the jury," Flip said cheerfully.

Ellery made a sound of exasperation and shook his head.

"Just like old times?" Flip suggested.

Tosh and Lenny were giggling in agreement as they marched Ellery along, arm-in-arm.

Watson was waiting on the front steps when they arrived back at Captain's Seat.

To his delight and Ellery's chagrin, unwarranted praise was heaped on his willful little noggin.

Tosh exclaimed. "Oh no. Look at that sweet little face! He thinks he's in trouble."

"He *is* in trouble." Ellery scowled at Watson, who hopped up on his hindlegs and placed his muddy paws on Ellery's thigh as though asking for clemency. Ellery lightly touched his index finger to Watson's nose. "You and I will talk later."

Watson licked Ellery's finger.

"Awww. You can't blame *him*," Lenny protested. "It was our idea."

"Oh, was that an actual *idea*?"

His friends laughed, not at all abashed, and apparently no longer alarmed at the idea of an axe-wielding murderer lurking in the night. Jack was not going to be happy to hear of the evening's adventure though, and Ellery winced inwardly at the idea of telling him.

After their impromptu night hike in forty-degree temps, everyone was only too happy to agree to the suggestion they leave their wet and muddy shoes at the door and settle down with hot drinks in front of the fireplace.

Ellery made hot buttered rum, which was his new favorite cold weather nightcap, and led the way to the library.

"I remember those 'before' pictures of the house," Tosh remarked as they crossed the great hall. "The way you feel about spiders, I didn't think you'd last the week."

Ellery laughed with everyone else, but the truth was, he hadn't been sure he'd last the first week, either. But he also didn't think he had a choice. He'd left his job, sold his brownstone, he'd—in the vernacular—put all his eggs in one very dusty basket. It would have taken more than a couple of broken windows and a whole lot of spiders, not to mention several species of lizards (all of which seemed to be using Captain's Seat as their headquarters) to drive him back to the mainland.

"How much did all this cost, Ellery?" Chelsea gazed up at the gigantic bronze shell that hung over the stone fireplace. The shell had once decorated the stern of a French frigate. "Restoring everything, I mean."

Flip muttered, "Jeez, Chels."

Chelsea glared at him. "You don't think Ellery wants to talk about what it took to renovate this place? It's all he's been doing for a year!"

Ellery intervened. "I didn't do all the renovations at once, and Jack helped me with a lot of the smaller stuff. It costs more than you think it will, that's for sure."

Tosh and Lenny laughed nervously. Chelsea said thoughtfully, "A lot of these antiques must be really valuable."

"Some of them, probably." Considering how much potentially valuable stuff had been collected over the centuries, it was kind of amazing that the house hadn't been vandalized or robbed like Skull House in the months following Great-aunt Eudora's death. Granted, Jack hadn't been watching over the island back then. And Skull House had been uninhabited a lot longer than Captain's Seat. Ellery, desperate for escape, had begun planning his move to Buck Island soon after he'd learned of his unexpected inheritance.

"Do you have a drawing room?" Tosh asked.

"A drawing room, a gallery, a library, a game room, a pantry, and a wine cellar off the main cellar."

"Was there a treasure trove of old wine in the wine cellar?"

"Nope. There wasn't a single bottle of wine or anything else in the wine cellar."

"Now *that's* disappointing," Lenny said.

"It would have all turned to vinegar anyway," Chelsea replied.

Flip said hopefully, "Game room as in video games?"

"Game room as in a room with a giant billiard table we'd need a crane to move."

The game room had not been included in the renovation plans, and it remained as untouched by time and cleaning products as an undiscovered Egyptian tomb.

They reached the library, Ellery found the light switch, and his guests gasped at the vision of the chipped and peeling mermaid figurehead suspended from the high ceiling of the long room.

Ellery gasped, too. But in his case, it had nothing to do with the mermaid, and everything to do with the narrow doorway usually discreetly hidden between the towering bookcases, but currently standing wide open.

CHAPTER SEVEN

"**W**hat? What's wrong?" Tosh demanded sharply, so maybe everyone was still a bit more on edge than he'd realized.

Ellery was quick to reassure. "I'm sure it's nothing. I was just surprised to see that panel open. The workmen must have forgotten about it when they left this morning." He nodded at the narrow doorway.

"Oh, my God. Is that a *secret passage*?"

Mugs were deposited on every available flat surface and the Scooby Gang—er, Ellery's friends—crowded around the entrance.

"Where does it lead to?"

"Have you already explored the whole thing?"

"Whoa, it's dark in there!"

"Can we go inside?"

Ellery absently listened to his friends while unobtrusively studying the shiny floor for mud or damp shoe prints. Though fixing drinks in the kitchen had supplied enough time for wet prints to evaporate, the imprint of muddy shoes would still be visible. He was relieved to see the floors and rugs looked untouched.

Anyway, if someone was lurking in that tunnel, Watson would be losing his mind right now...

Ellery watched Watson stick his nose into the gloom, sniffing energetically, and then letting out a full-body sneeze. Watson sneezed again. He quickly backed out, still sneezing loudly.

Ellery stepped over Watson, and joined the others. "This tunnel leads down to the cellar. But it may have originally had another branch that's blocked off now. There's a small hidden closet off the dining room which has another passage that might have led to an old greenhouse, which no longer exists."

"So it's a dead end?"

"Yes. The exit is sealed shut."

"Did you look for treasure?" Chelsea asked.

Ellery assumed Chelsea was kidding, and he laughed. "No. Not yet."

"But that's what your employee was saying, right?"

"My..."

"Nora," Tosh put in.

Chelsea shook her head. "No. The little man with the bow tie. He said something about the legend of the Dourdos Aquamarine."

Oh, right. Ellery remembered the reference but it hadn't made sense to him at the time—and still didn't, given that they'd been discussing the likelihood of Edwin Dolph popping up on Buck Island.

"That's the first I've ever heard of the Dourdos Aquamarine."

"*Oooh*," Tosh exclaimed. "We're going on a treasure hunt!"

Ellery laughed because, well, frankly, treasure hunting was in his DNA. But he had no idea what the Dourdos Aquamarine was, what the connection might be to the island—let alone to Captain's Seat. He wasn't even sure that's what Nora and Kingston had been hinting at. They could be cryptic when communicating with other lifeforms.

"Maybe? But—" He froze—they all froze—at the sound of the doorbell.

Ding-dong, psycho calling?

But Watson tore out of the room barking hysterically.

Arf! Arf! Arf!

It was a specific bark for a specific person.

"That's Jack." Ellery could hear the relief in his voice, which probably didn't do a lot to reassure his friends.

"Are you *sure* about that?" Tosh probably intended to sound teasing, though it didn't quite come off that way.

But Watson was never wrong about this, and he could be heard tags jingling as he raced down the hall, joyfully barking all the way. Ellery and the others followed.

When they reached the heavy wooden front door, Watson was jumping up and down on his hind legs as Jack rang the doorbell for a second time.

"Check first, Ellery!" Tosh urged.

Ellery was already peering through the peephole, and sure enough, the tiny figure at the end of the convex lens was Jack. The miniature Jack smoothed his hair, the only indication he felt any nervousness about meeting Ellery's old posse.

"It's okay. It's Jack."

"He doesn't have a key?" Somehow Chelsea managed to sound both surprised and skeptical.

"Yeah, he does. He's just being..."

Jack. Careful and courteous in front of Ellery's friends, in case they didn't know—in case Ellery didn't want them to know—the full scope of their relationship.

Ellery switched off the alarm, pulled back the wooden bolt, and opened the door. Before the space between door and frame was more than a few inches wide, Watson flew out and leaped into Jack's arms. Jack grunted.

Arms full of ecstatically wriggling puppy, Jack stood on the front stoop in a haze of yellow light. His sun-streaked brown hair was ruffled and his green-blue eyes were quizzical. He smiled at Ellery, then his gaze traveled to Ellery's companions, and his brows shot up. "I wasn't expecting a welcoming committee—"

Ellery cut him off with a kiss. Jack hung onto Watson with one arm and wrapped the other around Ellery, kissing him back. Jack's mouth smiled against Ellery's.

Watson began to wriggle free. He jumped down and circled Ellery and Jack, barking.

Ellery and Jack drew apart, and Ellery said, "Everybody, this is Jack."

"I should hope so!" Chelsea said, and everyone laughed. Introductions were made, Jack dutifully repeating names and committing faces to memory.

Ellery watched his friends smiling and shaking hands as they sized up Jack.

He knew what they were thinking—or at least part of what they were thinking. Jack was so completely different from anyone Ellery had ever dated, let alone from Brandon and Todd. Granted, they would consider that to be in Jack's favor.

"I didn't think there was any chance you'd make it back tonight," Ellery told Jack.

Jack's eyes crinkled at the corners when he smiled. "I told you I planned on driving out."

"You did, yeah, and I'm so glad to see you. Are you hungry?"

"I could eat something."

"Did you—?"

Jack read his mind without trouble. "There's no sign that Dolph made it onto the island."

There was a whole lot going unsaid there, but Ellery left it alone. There would be time to talk when they went upstairs.

He said instead, "Why don't you guys go ahead and have your drinks in the library. I'll fix Jack a plate and we'll join you in a couple of minutes."

Ellery's guests filed off to the library, and Ellery set about microwaving the plate of food he'd saved for Jack just in case.

"We just had a scare," he informed Jack as they waited for the food to heat. "The door to the passage in the library was open."

Jack's brows drew together. "Open?"

"I'm sure the workmen left it that way, but it definitely—"

"Did you double-check with Tony Brambilla?"

"At this time of night? There's absolutely no indication anyone entered the house. Well, I mean, except for the four people I invited."

Jack threw a cursory look at the clock on the wall, and grimaced. It was just after midnight. They both knew the good people of Pirate's Cove rolled up the cobblestones early this time of year.

Ellery added, "I'll double-check tomorrow, but workmen have been leaving lights on and doors unlocked and windows open since renovations began. It's just with everything else going on, it was a little...startling."

"I bet."

"What did you want to drink? Are you liable to get called out again?"

"Hopefully, no. I'll grab a beer." Jack opened the fridge.

The microwave dinged.

Ellery removed the plate as Jack poured his beer into a tall pilsner glass. Watson led the way as they joined everyone in the library where they were going through Tosh's box of photos.

Jack went over to examine the open panel. He briefly shone his flashlight inside the tunnel. He pushed the panel back into place, and sat beside Ellery on the long leather sofa. He picked up his plate of leftovers.

"This is a really nice room," Tosh told Ellery.

Ellery smiled. "Thanks. It's amazing what a subscription to *Better Homes and Gardens* can do."

Originally the library had not been on the list of planned renovations, but there had been quite a bit of paint left over, so Ellery had the room—which consisted almost entirely of towering bookshelves—repainted pristine white. The mermaid figurehead had been moved from the dining room to the library, and Ellery had sprung for having the antique rugs cleaned. He'd purchased a couple of large leather sofas and chairs, dragged a couple of carved wooden chests out of the cellar to use as tables, and called it a day. The end result was surprisingly charming.

"Hey, Chels, can I see that one?" Flip asked.

Chelsea seemed to come back to herself with a little start. "*Oh.* Sure." She handed Flip a snapshot. The insincerity of her smile as she handed the photo over caught Ellery's attention.

Was it his imagination? Or were there odd undercurrents flowing through their reunion?

Flip glanced at the photo and handed it to Ellery. "Ellery, this is a nice one of you and Noah."

Ellery took the photo, studied it with Jack.

Man, they had been young. He felt a pang at Noah's mischievous grin. Smart, talented, witty Noah...

Next to him, he felt Jack smile at the youthful Ellery and his rather alarming hair.

"I know," Ellery said. "I must have been going for *GQ* meets tumbleweed-in-a-tornado."

Jack chuckled but was tactful. "You were a very cute kid. Have you mentioned Noah before?"

"I don't think so. Noah died the year before we graduated."

Jack gave him a quick look. "Died?"

Chelsea gave a sudden laugh and held out another print out to Ellery. "Hey, Ell. You were talking about *The Cat and the Canary.*"

Ellery automatically reached for the snapshot and examined the ever-so-slightly blurry photo of the cast taking their bows.

Chelsea said, "I think that was closing night."

"Wow," Jack said very mildly, studying the players in their 1920s costumes.

This was met with knowing laughter.

"We got rave reviews for the costumes and sets," Ellery said.

"Ellery played Charlie," Chelsea said. "The villain. Not very convincingly."

Ellery shrugged. He couldn't argue with that. By that point in his education, he'd begun to be uncomfortably aware of his limitations as an actor.

Tosh put in, "I got to play Annabelle, but the part really should have gone to Chels."

Chelsea's smile was a little sour. "You were good. Anyway, you looked the part of the damsel in distress. I didn't."

Jack directed a thoughtful look her way.

"I was the escaped maniac known as the Cat," Flip chimed in. "And I think I was *very* convincing."

More laughter and jokey agreement. They continued to pass the photos around and reminisce as they finished their hot buttered rums.

Finally, Tosh smothered a yawn, and admitted, "I don't think I can keep my eyes open much longer."

"Same," Lenny said. "I don't want the night to end, but I'm going to be sleeping in Flip's lap in another minute."

"Time to call it a night," Flip agreed. He placed the lid on the photo box. "Tosh, you should take these up with you. You don't want Watson to accidentally knock the box over."

Watson, sound asleep on the sofa next to Ellery, never so much as twitched an eyelash at this aspersion.

"Oh. Okay." Tosh picked up the blue box. She smiled at Ellery. "This was *so* nice. Thanks for inviting us, Ell."

Ellery and Jack rose, Ellery hugged Tosh, and everyone wished each other good nights. Ellery's friends told Jack it was great to finally meet him. Jack told Ellery's friends it was great to finally meet *them*. Watson slept peacefully through it all.

As their guests' footsteps faded down the hall, Ellery and Jack smiled at each other.

"Why don't you go on up," Jack suggested. "I'm just going to make double sure everything's locked up for the night."

Ellery had taken care of that earlier in the evening, but he smiled. This was the way Jack was built. It was not about not trusting Ellery to protect his own hearth and home. It was about Jack not being able to relax until he was sure every "i" was dotted and every "t" crossed.

"Okay. Thanks, Jack."

"And I'll take Watson out."

"Oh, I think Watson's fine for the night," Ellery said grimly.

At the sound of his name, Watson, raised his head, blinked sleepily, and thumped his tail at Ellery.

"Uh oh," Jack said.

Ellery was sitting up in bed, absently stroking Watson's head and mulling over the evening, when Jack came upstairs about half an hour later.

"That took a while."

Jack nodded. "I know. I decided to check out the passageway." He shook his head. "I don't think anyone has been in there since the door was discovered. It's wet outside. There would be mud and tracks."

"Thanks for checking." Ellery cocked his head. "I guess the extra precautions mean that Dolph *is* on the island?"

Jack, stripping with speedy efficiency, grimaced. "A small craft was stolen from Point Judith this morning. It looks like it wrecked on the rocks beneath Skull House. But no body has been recovered so far."

Ellery blinked. "Could he have made it to shore?"

"It's possible. It's not *likely*. That water is rough and some of those rocks are razor sharp. But, yes, it is possible."

"Yikes."

"You said it." Jack stepped into a pair of sleep pants, pulled his navy LAPD sweatshirt over his head, and stepped into the bathroom.

"Possible but not likely," Ellery said to Watson. "But that's what they said about Dolph making it to the island at all."

Watson sighed heavily as though Ellery had kept him up for hours with uneasy speculations.

Jack finished up in the bathroom, crossed the bedroom, and crawled into bed. "I'm beat."

"It was a long day," Ellery agreed, as they moved into each other's arms.

"But a good day?" Jack kissed Ellery's forehead.

"Absolutely. It's great seeing everyone again." Ellery smiled at the memory of some of the evening's funnier moments.

"I like Tosh."

Ellery grinned. "Everyone likes Tosh."

"Flip's entertaining. Lenny's hard to read. Chelsea..."

"I know," Ellery agreed. "Something's up there. I'm not sure what. In fairness, I was probably least close to Chels, and I haven't seen much of her since college. I was kind of surprised she came this weekend."

Jack made a thoughtful sound.

"Have she and Tosh always rubbed each other the wrong way?"

"No. Not at all. They were close back in the day. This is something new. I think Tosh might be a little hurt by..."

"By?"

Ellery shrugged. He wasn't completely sure.

"Circumstances change. People change."

"Yes."

Jack regarded him, smiled a little. "You never know. Maybe the weekend will give them enough time and space to reconnect."

"Maybe?" Remembering those odd smiles of Chelsea's, Ellery couldn't help feeling doubtful. It was like Chelsea was enjoying having a secret that the rest of them didn't know. Which was not a very friendly attitude, frankly.

"In the meantime," Jack murmured, "let's you and I re-connect." He reached up and turned off the bedside lamp.

Ellery laughed.

CHAPTER EIGHT

"**O**h, no!" Tosh was scrolling through a cell phone text. "Belle's not coming!"

"*Oh, no*," Lenny and Flip chorused.

It was Friday morning and Ellery and his guests were having breakfast in the dining room. Jack had headed back to the village at the crack of dawn. Chelsea had not yet made an appearance.

Ellery's phone dinged as he, too, got a message from Belle. He scanned the apologetic text. "Damn. Her flight's been cancelled due to poor visibility. She says the soonest she could get another flight is tomorrow morning, which means she'd basically be arriving in time to leave with you on Sunday."

"But no," Lenny said. "We're five hours behind her. She'd be traveling back in time."

"Uh..." Flip said.

"No, but that's right."

Ellery said, "But the plane trip is about ten hours, so she'd be arriving late tomorrow night."

"And we leave on Sunday," Flip pointed out.

"Oh, my God," Chelsea said from the doorway. "Please don't tell me we're doing algebra word problems."

"Belle can't make it," Lenny told her.

Chelsea took a seat at the table and shuddered at the sight of the pan of quiche a few inches from her place setting. "Does anybody *really* think Belle was going to fly all the way from England for Ellery's housewarming?"

The others stared at her. Tosh and Ellery exchanged looks. Tosh said, "She certainly was. Why would she lie about it?"

Chelsea shrugged.

Ellery said, "She sounded to me like she planned on coming, but I can see why it doesn't make sense for her to fly over tomorrow."

"I just find it hard to believe she couldn't have caught an earlier flight if she'd really wanted to."

"Why are you being such a pill about this?" Tosh demanded. "You're making Ellery feel bad."

Well, not really. Ellery had spoken to Belle on the phone, so he knew she'd genuinely planned on coming. Belle was nearly as terrible an actor as he was. He was sorry, of course, because he and Belle always had fun playing off each other, and it had been a while.

"No offense, Ellery," Chelsea said. "It's just obvious Belle doesn't have time for any of us now. Why would she? She's marrying a viscount, for God's sake."

"*Wow*," Tosh said, and that seemed to sum it up for everyone.

Into the silence that followed, Ellery asked, "Would you like some coffee, Chelsea?"

"I would *love* some coffee."

Ellery rose, went into the kitchen to pour a cup of coffee. When he returned to the dining room, Flip was saying, "Okay, Oscar and Freddie just left Point Judith. Did you want me to drive to the harbor with you, Ell?"

"Sure."

Chelsea opened her mouth, but then closed it. Ellery wondered if she didn't want to be left alone with Tosh and Lenny who were currently treating her to a formidable cold silence.

Hopefully, they'd call a truce while he and Flip were gone because it was going to make for an awkward house party if his guests weren't speaking to each other.

"Jack's not at all what I pictured," Flip remarked on the drive to Pirate's Cove.

"What did you picture?"

"I'm not sure. But not someone quite so...serious."

"Well, he's not *always* serious," Ellery said, navigating an especially deep puddle in the road.

But come to think of it, yeah, Jack joked around, sure; he had a good sense of humor and he could be playful and fun, but he was a serious guy.

"No, of course not," Flip said quickly. "And he seems very nice."

"He is *very* nice."

"He's very alert."

Ellery glanced briefly from the road to Flip. "Yes. He's—he pays attention."

"He watches everything," Flip said thoughtfully. "In fact, even if I didn't know he was a cop, I'd wonder if he was a cop. You can feel him observing—observing and assessing the situation all the time."

"Can you?" Ellery said neutrally. He wasn't sure where this was going. He wanted his friends to like Jack, but it was their loss if they didn't. It would not affect Ellery's feelings for Jack in the least.

He said, "Jack was a homicide detective with LAPD before he moved to Pirate's Cove."

"Was he? I'll bet he was good at it."

"He doesn't talk much about his life back then, but I'm sure he was. He's a good police chief."

Flip smiled suddenly, "He gets this expression when he's looking at you. I don't know how to explain it. It's something in his eyes. Like looking at you is a relief."

Ellery chuckled. "That's only because right now I'm not snooping into anything he wants me to stay out of. That's gotta be a *big* relief."

Flip assented and added, "Brandon used to look at you like you were a juicy piece of steak!"

They both laughed.

They had been late leaving the house, so by the time they reached the harbor, the ferry had docked and passengers were disembarking. The air seemed significantly colder from the day before, and it had started to drizzle again. The drizzle was getting a bit slushy. Ellery couldn't help thinking the dark clouds hanging heavily in the sky promised more and worse weather.

Oscar and Freddie were already on the quay. Unlike the day before, the crossing had been relatively smooth, and they seemed unfazed by their trip. Freddie was signing autographs for two women in brightly colored raincoats, while Oscar looked on with a sardonic smile.

Tall, athletic, and handsome, Freddie was forever getting cast as rogue cops or dashing criminals. In real life, he was easygoing, gregarious, and laidback to the point of indolence. He was also engagingly modest (or just honest) about his surprisingly successful career in Hollywood—and more than happy to help his friends whenever possible.

Oscar was tall and thin and intense-looking. He practically crackled with nervous energy. His hair was black, as were his eyes, and in college had tried out a variety of mustaches, from handlebar to pencil thin, none of which had suited him. He had since settled on a mustache-goatee combo, and *that* look, he rocked. Midway through Tisch, he had changed majors, moving from the Institute of Performing Arts to the Maurice Kanbar Institute of Film & Television, but their small circle of friends had remained unbroken. He now worked as an archivist at the UCLA Film and Television Archive.

Ellery and Flip waved down to Oscar and Freddie. Oscar nudged Freddie, and Freddie hastily sketched a quick salute to them and finished up with his fans. They grabbed their suitcases and hauled them noisily up the cement ramp.

There were half-hugs and smacks on the back all around, and then Oscar pulled out a copy of the *Narragansett Times*. Blazoned across the top of the paper was the banner headline,

Edwin Dolph Found Not Guilty by Reason of Insanity Escapes Psychiatric Hospital.

"Oh, *that*," Ellery said.

Freddie laughed. Oscar echoed, "*Oh, that???* It says he's somewhere on your island!"

"It's not like I invited him," Ellery objected.

"My God. You should *see* that house," Flip interrupted. "It's like it was designed by the ancestor of whoever did *Pirates of the Caribbean*."

"Movie or theme park attraction?" Oscar was instantly distracted.

"Theme park attraction," Flip answered promptly.

"We can't leave you alone for a minute, Page!" Freddie put his arms around Flip and Oscar, urging them forward. "Let's get out of the rain."

The rain *was* coming down harder now, bullets of wet bouncing off the cement and railings and choppy surface of the water.

They jog-walked the luggage to Ellery's VW, stuffed the suitcases in the cramped backseat with Oscar and Freddie, and headed back to Captain's Seat, everyone—as usual—talking at once.

Freddie, in typically generous fashion, had upgraded Oscar's ticket to first class so they could travel together, and it was soon apparent the two of them had had a pleasant and well-lubricated flight across the country.

After a lively travelogue, which heavily featured a cute air attendant who was also an aspiring actress, Oscar pulled out his newspaper again.

"Forty-year-old Edwin Dolph, who was found not guilty by reason of insanity for the 2019 axe murders of his father, Retired Judge Barclay Dolph; his mother, Judge Candace Whitman Dolph; and his sister, Clementine Dolph, escaped late Wednesday night from the Rhode Island State Psychiatric Hospital (RISPH), located in the Roosevelt Benton facility on the Cranston campus. As Ellery would say, *yikes*!"

Flip asked, "Ellery, do you still say *yikes*?"

"Yikes," Ellery said on cue. "Did I used to say that a lot?"

The other three laughed, and then Oscar continued to read. *"Authorities have not ruled out the possibility that Dolph might have received inside help in formulating his escape.* Not good. *Although originally considered high risk, in recent years Dolph*...hmm...yada yada yada..."

"What's the yada yada yada part?" Ellery asked.

"I guess the last time anything like this happened was 1907."

"Frank Weeden," Ellery agreed.

"Uh, right. It says the Dolph family used to own a summer house on the island, but it sounds like that was way before this guy's time."

Flip asked, "Does it say anything about the Dourdos Aquamarine?"

"The what?" Freddie asked.

Oscar scanned the paper. "Nope." He resumed reading. "*RI State Police Colonel Giordano has warned that Dolph, while not convicted of homicide due to his mental state, may still pose a risk to the public. Citizens are advised not to approach him and to contact authorities immediately.* Ya think?"

Freddie said, "I think we should keep this from the girls."

Three pairs of accusing gazes—Ellery scowled into the rearview mirror—met this announcement, and Freddie protested, "Why would we want to ruin their weekend?"

Oscar said, "Because it's not the 1950s, Fred. They have a right to know what's going on."

"But nothing's going on! It's typical doom and gloom media speculation."

"It's not speculation that a dangerous mental patient escaped and is maybe running loose on this island."

"*Maybe*," Freddie stressed. "Or maybe not. I seriously doubt even a crazy person is going to try camping out in this weather. I bet he faked the cops out and is hiding in plain sight in New York right now."

"Okay, wait a minute," Ellery interjected. "According to Jack, they found the wreckage of the boat Dolph stole on the other side of the island. There's a high probability he drowned, but they didn't find a body. So."

Flip stared at him. "Talk about keeping things from people."

Ellery made a face. "I only found out late last night after everyone was in bed."

"As far as I remember, we all had breakfast together."

"I got distracted by Tosh and Chelsea, and then we were running late. It just slipped my mind."

"An *escaped axe-murderer* slipped your mind?"

"What about Tosh?" Freddie scrunched forward to better hear.

"She and Chelsea are getting on each other's nerves," Flip said.

"Sure. And now you want to stress them out even more by telling them there could be an axe-murderer wandering around the island."

Ellery sighed.

"I don't think it's going to stress them out as much as you imagine," Flip said. "They were *totally* enjoying appearing in last night's episode of *Eerie Indiana*. We all were. Right, Ellery?"

"Wellllll..." Ellery said.

"But seriously."

Ellery said, "But seriously, Freddie, we can't hide this from them. Even if it wasn't already way too late."

"I'm just thinking of the girls," Freddie said.

"From your time machine," joked Flip.

Freddie grumpily shoved away Oscar's duffel bag, which had slid onto his shoulder, and sat back in his seat.

Oscar grinned and nudged Freddie with his elbow. "Chivalry is not dead so long as you're around, my friend."

"Ha!" Freddie said.

CHAPTER NINE

Tosh and Freddie's divorce, a year after they married, came as a surprise to no one but Freddie.

What *had* surprised everyone, or at least the people who knew them well, was how they'd ever got together in the first place.

Or rather, what had convinced Tosh to plight her troth to a big goof like Freddie.

Because it was no mystery what had initially attracted her. Freddie was handsome and fun and generous. He was a surprisingly decent actor, if limited in range, and—most surprising of all, given the way girls threw themselves at him—he had been absolutely devoted to Tosh.

Equally, it was no mystery as to what had initially attracted Freddie to Tosh. She was lovely and lively and smart. She laughed easily at Freddie's terrible jokes. She was a very good actress—she had that instant likeability factor both onstage and off. And she had a trust fund. Not that money had ever been an issue for Freddie. His parents were wealthy, too.

But what had worked so effortlessly in the context of college and a strong supportive circle of friends had quickly crumbled under the strains of independent adult life. Ellery had no idea about what had finally driven a wedge between them. The most Tosh had said on the subject was something to the effect of she and Freddie having "different interior lives".

Ellery wasn't sure if that meant they held different religious beliefs or something else. He hadn't wanted to pry. Like the rest of their mob, he was relieved that Freddie and Tosh had split up as easily and amicably as they'd come together. There had been no need to choose sides (not that there was any question whose side Ellery would have been on). And the truth was, everyone was too busy chasing their own star to spend a lot of time dissecting the end of a relationship that they'd all secretly suspected wouldn't last anyway.

Freddie had moved to Hollywood where every few months he popped into the pages of *People* magazine with a stunning new actress on his arm. Tosh had eventually given up the idea of a career in acting and taken the prestigious job as director of special events for the Roundelay Theater Group in Manhattan. She dated regularly but not steadily, and showed little interest in "settling down" with anyone but her cat, Waldo.

Which was why Ellery hadn't thought twice about inviting both Freddie and Tosh to his weekend house party.

And his confidence was not misplaced.

When he shepherded Oscar and Freddie into the library where Tosh, Lenny, Chelsea, and Watson had taken up residence before the fireplace, everyone greeted each other like the old friends they were.

"Hello, Beautiful," Freddie said to Tosh, giving her a big hug. "Long time, no see."

"Hey you!" Tosh returned the hug.

And that was that.

A heck of a lot less painless than the awkward smiles and near collision of noses when Oscar and Tosh went to kiss hello. In fact, that *Hello, Stranger!* kiss was so poorly executed—and Tosh and Oscar were so clearly flustered by the misfire—that Ellery found himself mentally reviewing everything Tosh had ever said on the subject of Oscar.

It wasn't much.

Meanwhile, Freddie had moved on to greet Chelsea, putting his hands up in a *don't shoot* gesture, and saying, "I know, I know. I owe you an email!"

Chelsea laughed and rolled her eyes. "Lucky for you, I forgot I even wrote you."

That wasn't something Freddie often heard. He glanced back and his eyes widened. "*Whoa*, Chelse. You look..."

Chelsea lifted her chin, shook back her hair, and waited with a confident and cheeky smile.

"Fantastic," Freddie concluded. He winked at her and turned to Lenny. "Hey, Bewitched! How long has it been?"

Ellery didn't hear Lenny's reply. He'd caught a glimpse of Tosh's expression, and he was pretty sure it matched his own, although maybe for different reasons.

The instant transformation of Chelsea from, well, the worst version of herself to a rom-com heroine was kind of jaw-dropping. A makeover was one thing. This was like a personality transplant.

It was just...weird.

Meanwhile, Watson, generally a social animal, had apparently woken up on the wrong side of Ellery's bed. He jumped on the leather ottoman and began to bark excitedly.

Arf! Arf! Arf!

He did not appear to be barking at anyone or anything in particular. It was more of a generalized and uncharacteristic agitation.

"*Dog*," Lenny protested, covering her ears with her hands.

Arf! Arf! Arf!

Flip grinned at Ellery. "It looks like Watson wants to make a speech."

Arf! Arf! Arf!

Ellery said apologetically, "I think he's probably over-stimulated. I'll take him for a walk. Watson, want to go for a—"

Say no more! Say no more! Well, actually, it was Arf! Arf! Arf! *Arf! Arf! Arf!* But the gist was the same. Watson leaped from the ottoman and raced for the hall. Ellery followed, leaving Oscar and Freddie to fill everyone in on the details of their trip and the alarming news from Point Judith.

Watson was impatiently jumping up and down at the front door. Ellery opened the door and Watson charged outside. Oddly, he did not take off for the meadow, which was their usual walk. Instead, he raced around to the back of the house, still barking like a foxhound when it hits a line.

"What the heck," Ellery murmured, striding after.

The air smelled of woodsmoke and winter. The hard rain had turned to feathery-soft snow, and the snow was starting to stick. Ellery eyed it uneasily. A little snow would be nice and cozy. A lot of snow would be a huge problem and probably mean cancelling Saturday night's housewarming party.

When he reached the back garden, he found Watson running up and down the length of the house, snuffling the frozen ground and barking excitedly.

Ellery felt a flicker of alarm, but wasn't it far more likely some small creature like a squirrel or a raccoon was hoping to take up residence for the winter? More likely than, say, a dangerous mental hospital escapee was trying to...

What?

Burrow under the house in search of a secret entrance?

Of course, that didn't mean such an entrance couldn't exist. In fact, there was a strong possibility there was another point of entry somewhere on the grounds. It was a very large house. It had a lot of secrets.

Ellery followed the path Watson was cutting through the browned and dormant flower beds. He was searching for any sign that someone had walked this way recently, but there were no prints in the sodden ground, no crushed plants, no smooshed grass.

Of course not. Because Edwin Dolph was floating somewhere in the surf beneath Skull House.

It was a grim thought.

Ellery whistled to Watson, but Watson remained intent on whatever he imagined he was about to corner beneath the house. So Ellery walked on, trusting that Watson would soon follow after.

A few feet from the wood pile, he stopped in his tracks. The hair on the back of his neck stood up. The hatchet he had used to split the kindling the day before, the hatchet he had left lodged in the low tree stump, was gone.

"What the..."

Slowly, he walked up to the stump and stared down. Beneath the light dusting of snow, he could see the deep groove where the hatchet was usually wedged. There was no hatchet.

He took a step back and circled the stump. He walked up and down the woodpile, walked a few feet out. There was no sign of the hatchet.

Ellery let out a long breath. He pulled his phone out and called Jack's cell.

"Hey," Jack said. "How's it going?"

"Well, it's going okay," Ellery said slowly.

"Oscar, Freddie, and Belle make it safely?"

"Belle's flight was canceled, but Oscar and Freddie are here at the house."

Jack's tone changed. "Everything okay? You sound a little..."

"This is probably nothing."

"Okay," Jack said cautiously.

"But you know the hatchet we use to chop kindling? The one we keep stuck in the stump next to the woodpile? It's gone."

"It's gone," Jack repeated. There was no particular inflection in his tone.

"I know I left it out here. But there's no sign of it now."

Jack made a thoughtful sound.

"I didn't put it in the garden shed and forget about it. I didn't carry it into the house with the kindling. It was definitely here yesterday."

"Okay."

"We don't have any neighbors to borrow tools without asking. I know an owl didn't carry it off. So, what happened to it?"

"I'm not sure."

I'm not sure sounded like maybe Jack did have a theory.

Ellery said cautiously, "I'm overreacting, aren't I? You've found Dolph?"

Jack said slowly, "No. We haven't found Dolph yet. You're not necessarily overreacting, but there could be a benign explanation. For one thing, you've got a house full of practical jokers. Right?"

A wave of relief washed over Ellery. *Of course.* Of course that was the most obvious explanation. Either Tosh, Lenny, or (more likely) Chelsea had hidden the hatchet to freak him out. This was exactly the type of prank they'd used to pull on each other.

Granted, they'd never been in circumstances quite like these.

But it wouldn't have mattered if they had.

"*Yes.*" Ellery gave a relieved laugh. "You're right. That's exactly what this is. I'm being ridiculous."

"No, you're not. You're being cautious, which I completely approve of. Better safe than sorry."

"True. But they're *my* friends. I should have thought of that. It's the obvious explanation."

"No worries." Jack's tone changed again. "Other than the case of the disappearing hatchet, everything okay?"

"Yep. Everything's fine. I just brought the guys back from the ferry a little while ago. Watson was acting out, so I thought I'd take him for a quick walk and then I'll see what everyone wants to do. Any chance you'll make dinner tonight?"

"I can't promise, but yes, there's a chance."

"Do you think Dolph made it to shore?"

"That boat was smashed to pieces. I don't think so. And the officers who grew up on this island don't think so. But until we've got a body, I'm not taking anything for granted. Please be extra vigilant on your walk. Maybe don't go too far from the house."

Ellery sighed. "Right. Well, be careful. It's snowing, by the way. For real."

"I know. I'll talk to you later."

"Love you," Ellery said.

He heard the smile in Jack's, "Love you, too."

As Ellery disconnected, he realized that the blessed and sudden silence surrounding him was the result of Watson no longer barking. He looked around. Watson sat at his feet, head cocked, doing his best impersonation of a good dog.

"What was all that about?"

Watson brightened, wagged his tail.

"You're turning into the little dog who cried wolf. I don't know when I should take you seriously."

Watson flung himself on the snowy grass, rolled over twice, and jumped up in the air.

"That's what I'm afraid of," Ellery said. "Come on. Let's go back inside and show Freddie and Oscar where they're sleeping tonight."

"**H**ey, Ellery. I hear congratulations are in order," Freddie said when there was a pause in the conversation.

Ellery and his houseguests were having a light lunch in the dining room: wine, tapas, cheese, and charcuterie boards. Through the tall windows they could see the snow lazily drifting down, casually, as if in afterthought, carpeting the garden.

"Thanks." Ellery, topping up Lenny's wine glass, smiled. His smile froze when Freddie added, "I couldn't believe it when I read in *Variety* you were coming back for the *Happy Halloween* reboot."

"What?" Tosh stared at Ellery. "You haven't said a word."

"That's terrific," Flip said. "But I thought you said you wouldn't—you weren't—"

Lenny interjected, "I thought you hated those movies?"

"Well, *that's* a coup," Chelsea said. She sounded more disbelieving than impressed.

"I know." Ellery directed that mostly at Tosh. "I have mixed feelings about it. But I need the money."

"Good for you," Oscar said heartily. He glanced at Tosh.

"I think it's great," Freddie said. "And Black Palace is putting a ton of money into this. This is going to be great for you."

"I hope so."

"I *know* so," Freddie said.

"What does Jack say?" Tosh asked.

Chelsea responded, "Why should Jack have a say in anything?"

"Because they're getting married, Chels!"

"So what? Is Ellery supposed to give up his career—"

"Girls, girls!" Freddie looked taken aback. "It's between Jack and Ellery, right?"

Lenny said earnestly, "Ell, if this is what you want, I'm totally happy for you. I'm just surprised because I kind of thought your whole reason for coming here was you were done with acting and-and all that."

"I need the money," Ellery repeated wearily. "That's the only reason I agreed. It's a sweet deal and a small role, and hopefully it's not going to disrupt anything because I'm very happy with my life right now."

A small silence followed.

Then Flip picked up his wine glass. "Hey, personally, I think Ellery is making the right choice. We all know opportunities like this come around once in a lifetime. He'd be crazy *not* to jump at it. We should toast to Ellery's success." He rose.

Ellery said uncomfortably, "Really, that's not—"

He was firmly ignored. Tosh, Chelsea, Lenny, Freddie and Oscar rose also.

"Here's to the return of Noah Street," Flip said. "Long may he run—"

"Screaming," supplied Lenny.

This was followed by laughter and clinking glasses.

CHAPTER TEN

The first documented owner of the legendary emerald-cut aquamarine known as the Dourdos Aquamarine was the French Emperor Louis XVI. The gem disappeared during the French Revolution but was acquired by Cornelius Vanderbilt following World War I for his wife, wealthy socialite Grace Vanderbilt.

At the time the gem weighed 112.92 carats and had natural, aquatic blue colors. Delicate bands, accented with 130 micro pavé-set diamonds, encircled the stone in its 18k white gold pendant mounting.

Ellery was reading the Wikipedia entry on the Dourdos Aquamarine.

Tosh and Freddie and Oscar had attempted to take Watson for a walk, but Watson was having none of it. He was lying on the sofa between Ellery and Lenny, deigning to allow Lenny to scratch his tummy.

Flip, in a chair by the fireplace, was skimming Ellery's well-worn copy of 1955's *Historic and Architectural Resources of Buck Island, Rhode Island* by Philby Hammond, Esq.

The book, as Ellery knew well, was an idiosyncratic but surprisingly useful treasure trove of information about the island's history. Particularly its more recent history. Flip was hoping to learn something useful about the Dolph family, especially any possible connection between the Dolphs and the Dourdos Aquamarine.

Ellery wasn't exactly sure what had decided his friends to help him in his "sleuthing". He hadn't really *planned* on any sleuthing, since as far as any of them knew, there was no mystery to be solved. Certainly, not a mystery that involved him or his guests. The fact that this "case" his friends kept referring to did not actually exist, didn't seem to discourage them at all.

"*Oh, my God*!" Chelsea, lying on the sofa on the other side of the room, burst out laughing. "You guys, you *have* to see this." She held out her cell phone to Flip.

Flip sighed, pushed his reading glasses up, and got to his feet. He took the phone, studied the screen for a couple of minutes, and laughed reluctantly.

"What?" Lenny looked up from K.K. Peabody's *Ghosts of Buck Island*.

Flip said, "It's a teaser on YouTube for the *Happy Halloween* reboot."

"Lemme see!" Lenny abandoned Watson and her book to join Flip in front of the fireplace. She watched for a couple of seconds and then started giggling. "That's *brilliant*."

"Oh, no." Ellery knew *brilliant* was going to inevitably translate into *highly embarrassing*.

"Oh, *yes*." Chelsea gave an evil chuckle.

Lenny was still giggling as she handed Chelsea's phone to Ellery. "It's actually really fun," she said consolingly.

Ellery studied the blurred first frame of the trailer, sighed, pressed play.

The wide-eyed wild-haired twenty-three-year-old version of himself appeared, saying with mechanical earnestness, "Guys, hear me out. I know it sounds crazy. But it *is* possible!"

Ellery groaned in pain as the retro-style voice-over proclaimed, "IT'S NOT ONLY POSSIBLE, IT'S HAPPENING," followed by quick cuts of the reboot's stars Fallon Provost and Billie Watson running through a foggy graveyard, kissing in a crypt, and splattered in blood, screaming. Lots of blood, LOTS of screaming.

Since filming had not yet started, these promo clips might not even make it into the final film, but they were effective. The final frame, in the original, now-dated film typography, promised a release date of the Halloween after next.

"It's *way* too early to start promo," Ellery objected. He was already starting to get cold feet.

Lenny snatched the phone back. "Here, I have to see that again."

Guys, hear me out. I know it sounds crazy. But it is possible! A tiny, tinny voice cried from the bowels of YouTube.

"You had Timothée Chalamet hair before there ever was a Timothée Chalamet." She was giggling again.

"Before—! How the heck old do you think I *am*?" Ellery protested.

Chelsea said, "Oh, my *God*. What if they make Fallon's Noah Junior grow his hair out like the original Noah?"

"He could just wear a wig," Flip said. "Something similar to what Harpo Marx wore?"

"You are so dead," Ellery said.

Flip laughed.

"Isn't that the new franchise title?" Chelsea inquired. *"Happy Halloween! You Are SO Dead*?"

Eventually, they ran out of material for their standup routines and everyone settled back into their various reading and viewing, interrupted only by an occasional snicker from Chelsea.

Ellery scanned the rest of the Wikipedia entry.

In 1927 the aquamarine was stolen by twenty-four-year-old Cyril Dolph, who had worked briefly as a chauffeur for the Vanderbilts. Although it was believed that Dolph had a confederate within the household staff, no link was ever proven. Two days after the theft, Dolph was arrested in Rhode Island; however, the pendant was never recovered.

In 1932, Dolph was convicted and sentenced to prison. He died a month later of pneumonia. The Dourdos Aquamarine remains missing to this day.

"Hey, I found something on the Dourdos Aquamarine," Ellery announced. "There's a Wikipedia entry on it."

Ignoring the aspersions cast on the source of information, he read the Wikipedia article out loud.

"Okay, he was captured in Rhode Island," Flip said. "But does that mean *here*? Or does that mean the mainland?"

"It doesn't say." Ellery considered. "But I know who probably has the answer to that question."

Nora picked up on the first ring. "I was just about to phone you."

Ellery felt a spark of alarm as images of leaking roofs, leaking windows, and flooded floors flashed through his mind. "Is everything okay?"

"Oh yes. Everything's fine," Nora assured him. "However, I sent Kingston home before lunch. I think we should probably close the shop for the rest of the day. We haven't had a single customer since yesterday morning, and given the weather..."

Ellery, standing at the kitchen window and watching the back garden shrubs and architecture slowly lose all shape and definition beneath the snow, sighed. "Yeah. I'm sure you're right."

Nora interpreted the sigh correctly. "After all, the snow may stop tonight."

"Is that what the National Weather Service says?"

"Er...no."

"I figured."

Nora said, "To be honest, this is starting to feel a bit like the storm we had back in 1978."

"Wasn't that the most snow Rhode Island received in recorded history?"

Nora made another of those little hemming-hawing sounds.

"Terrific."

"What are the chances of another historic snowstorm?" Nora asked reasonably.

"I'm starting to think, pretty high. Do you feel I should cancel the party now? I don't want people driving out here in risky conditions."

"There's plenty of time to make that call tomorrow," Nora said. "It's not as though people will be turning down other engagements. We'll all be snowed in, if it comes to it."

"True, I guess. I did want to ask you something. I was reading up on the Dourdos Aquamarine—"

"*Oh!*" It was the tone of someone who has received an unexpected gift. "Excellent!"

"Do you know where in Rhode Island Cyril Dolph was when he was arrested for stealing the pendant?"

Nora did not question what some might consider an odd inquiry. "He was arrested in a little inn in Newport. The inn is gone now, sadly."

"So not on the island?"

"No." Nora added, "*However.*"

"However?"

"At the time, it was rumored that he had been to the island the day before. That was never substantiated, but the Dolph home in Pirate's Cove was searched top-to-bottom."

"And?"

"There was no sign of the Dourdos Aquamarine."

"Which doesn't mean..."

"It doesn't mean anything either way," Nora agreed. "What matters in this case is what Edwin Dolph might *think* it means."

Ellery mulled that over. "Do you have reason to think Edwin believes the aquamarine is on the island?"

Nora admitted, "I know very little about Edwin. Sadly, he lost his marbles when he was quite young."

"Yeah, I'm pretty sure that's not a medical term."

"I'm pretty sure you're right. However, while I know little of that unfortunate man, I can tell you that Dolphs have been sneaking back to the island to hunt for the aquamarine since the 1940s. Which would lead one to conclude that the family knows something that no one else does."

"Not enough," Ellery pointed out. "If they're coming back, generation after generation, to search for it."

"Not enough," Nora agreed.

"Are you aware of any connection between the Dolphs and Captain's Seat?"

"None that I'm aware of. It would be unlikely. The Dolphs and the Pages would have traveled in very different social circles."

"Would they? So would the Shandys and the Pages, but there's for sure some Venn diagrams going on there."

Nora said unhappily, "I do wish you wouldn't encourage those people, dearie."

Ellery let that pass. "So, there wouldn't be any reason for Edwin Dolph to believe the Dourdos Aquamarine is hidden somewhere at Captain's Seat?"

"No. I think it's very unlikely Cyril would have chosen Captain's Seat as a hiding place. In 1927 the house was full of family and servants. No, if Cyril did conceal the pendant on the island, it's somewhere in Pirate's Cove. My best guess would be the tunnels."

"Ah."

"Although, I imagine the Dolphs have scoured them pretty extensively by now." Nora added, "But you don't need to worry about Edwin Dolph showing up at Captain's Seat. It seems more and more likely he drowned before he could reach the island."

"But they still haven't found his body."

"Nnno. But that's not so surprising at this time of year and in this weather. There's a very strong undertow along that stretch of coastline."

"True," Ellery said doubtfully.

Nora said bracingly, "You just enjoy this time with your friends. And if the weather cooperates, we'll see you tomorrow at the housewarming."

"Okay. Close up and get out of there, Nora. I don't like the idea of you walking home in this weather."

Nora reassured him she would leave shortly. She sounded genuinely amused at the notion she could come to any harm in a little old snowstorm, and clicked off.

Ellery no sooner put his phone away when it rang. He pulled his phone out, assuming Nora had further thoughts on "the case," but it was Jack's photo that flashed up. He sighed, pressed accept.

"It's okay. I figured you'd be stuck in town tonight."

"Actually, I'm on my way over. I'm just checking to see if you need anything."

He was unprepared for that feeling of sweeping relief. Why was *he* so on edge? It's not like he *really* thought Edwin Dolph was lurking outside, so why the mounting unease?

"You're on your way?"

"Yep. We've decided to call off the search for now. The weather conditions are deteriorating fast. Do you need anything?"

Ellery gave a quick thought. They had plenty of food, plenty of drink, plenty of water, enough firewood to see them through the weekend, candles, matches, extra blankets, a first aid kit... Hopefully, the power would not go out, but if it did, they were reasonably prepared.

"Just you getting home safely."

"I'll see you in a bit," Jack promised.

CHAPTER ELEVEN

Ellery returned to the library where Watson was telling Freddie, Oscar, and Tosh what he thought of people who went for walks without him.

"We tried to bring you," Tosh pointed out. "You didn't want to come."

Watson responded to the word *come*, by hurling himself into Tosh's arms. She staggered back and Oscar reached to steady her. They smiled into each other's eyes, and Watson gave his seal of approval by planting a wet one on Tosh's mouth.

Tosh squeaked in dismay, and everyone laughed.

Ellery happened to glance at Freddie's face. Freddie was laughing too, but there was something in his eyes. A flicker of sadness?

Or maybe he imagined it, because the next instant Freddie had seated himself beside Chelsea, resting his arm behind her shoulders on the sofa back. Chelsea beamed up at him.

Ellery said, "Okay, now that I have you all together, which one of you comedians took the hatchet I use for chopping kindling?"

Silence. Blank faces all around.

Then Chelsea laughed. "Seriously? With an axe murderer on the loose? That's just mean, Ellery."

"I'm not kidding."

His friends looked at each other and then started laughing and shaking their heads.

"*Hey*," Ellery protested. "I'm serious."

Chelsea rolled her eyes. Freddie glanced around the room. "Okay. Ellery doesn't think it's funny, so..."

"Uh oh. Detective Bolton's on the case," Flip teased.

Freddie was unamused. Oscar said, "Freddie's right. We're a little old for this."

"Ouch." Chelsea sighed heavily. "Okay. I'll play along. When did you first notice the axe was missing, Ellery?"

Lenny was looking at Flip. Flip was looking at Lenny. Ellery knew those looks of old, but, also as of old, he was not sure about what they were silently communicating. They knew something. Or thought they did.

"I noticed when I took Watson out. After we got back from meeting the ferry."

"Watson, didn't go to meet the ferry," Chelsea pointed out.

"Chels," Freddie murmured.

Chelsea made a face. "Sorry. It's just—the idea that one of *us* would swipe his hatchet for a joke is a little weird."

"But not out of character," Tosh said pointedly.

Chelsea flushed. "The difference is, Tosh, *this* isn't funny."

"Agreed."

Tosh and Chelsea glared at each other.

"Okay," Ellery said quickly. "I don't want to start a big argument. If you all say you didn't take it, then I accept your word."

How was that the wrong thing to say? Yet, Chelsea's face grew tighter.

Oscar said, "But what does that mean? Where did the hatchet go?"

"I must have mislaid it."

This got frowns all around. Flip said, "Yeah. No. *Now* I'm worried."

Freddie said slowly, "So the hatchet really *is* missing."

"I wouldn't make it up," Ellery said.

Watson, sensing a change in the atmosphere, wriggled out of Tosh's arms and went to Ellery, pawing at his leg.

Tosh said, "Could it have fallen from wherever and now it's under the snow?"

"Sure."

More looks of alarm from his friends.

"You trying to reassure us is the most frightening thing of all," Flip informed him.

Ellery huffed in exasperation, and said, "Let's just leave it for now. I'm sure it will turn up. Anyway, Jack's on his way home, so how about we start dinner? I bought a bunch of pizza crusts and I thought I'd make sauce and you can pick your toppings."

The change of subject clearly came as a relief.

"That's a *great* idea!" Tosh enthused.

Flip agreed. "Remember our old Monday night pizza parties?"

"I don't think I've ever enjoyed a Monday as much since," Chelsea admitted.

It occurred to Ellery he had no idea what Chelsea did for a living. It also occurred to him that the ripple effect of doubt, created by the news of the missing hatchet, still lingered.

Jack arrived as the final slices of jalapeno were being judiciously applied to the last pizza.

"This looks industrious—and delicious." Jack put his arm around Ellery and they exchanged a quick hello kiss. "Hello, you rascal," Jack greeted Watson, who was leaping higher and higher in an attempt to get some acknowledgement from his hero.

"Jack, this is Freddie and Oscar." Ellery made the introductions.

Jack shook hands with Freddie and Oscar.

Oscar said, "So, you're the famous Jack."

"World renowned," Jack said gravely.

Freddie said, "Should we call you 'Chief'?"

Jack's expression grew quizzical. "Jack's fine."

"Ellery says you used to work Homicide for LAPD. Can I pick your brain later, Jack?"

"Sure."

Ellery thought Jack looked pleasant but unenthused.

Flip asked if there was any news regarding Edwin Dolph, and Jack admitted there was not and that the search had been called off for the evening.

"What are the chances you'll be able to resume tomorrow?" Ellery said,

Jack grimaced. "We'll see. The weather service is predicting a possible eighteen inches over the next thirty hours."

This news received gasps of dismay.

"Oh, *no*," Lenny said. "We're snowed in!"

"Not yet," Jack said. "But, yes, the ferry stopped running an hour ago."

Ellery's friends looked at each other in alarm.

"I have to be back on the set on Monday," Freddie said. "We've got the November sweeps this month!"

Jack nodded noncommittally. "We'll see how it goes." Which was a very cop-like thing to say and not really all that comforting.

"On the bright side," Ellery said quickly, "we've got pizza in the oven, plenty of wine, plenty of beer, and warm beds for everyone. It could be worse, right?"

"Heck, yeah," Tosh said. "I mean, if we have to be stranded, "I can't think of a better bunch of fellow refugees."

"I'll drink to that." Oscar held up his wine glass.

"Here, here," Freddie clinked his glass against Tosh's.

And, in fact, it was a very lively and pleasant evening, full of recollections and laughter.

Of course, it was hard to go wrong with beer and pizza—or wine and pizza. And there was plenty of everything, including a large green salad and chocolate-raspberry gelato for dessert.

Twice during the meal, the lights flickered and went out, but each time they came right back on, followed by a collective sigh of relief.

"Even if the power goes out, we've got plenty of flashlights and candles and firewood," Ellery reassured.

"Do you think the power's going to go out?" Lenny asked Jack.

Interestingly, even though Ellery's friends hadn't known Jack long, they already recognized him as a point of authority and accurate information. But then, that was Jack. He exuded competence and reliability. Qualities Ellery hadn't particularly valued in a potential partner until he'd met Jack.

Jack, always measured, replied, "I think it's likely we'll lose power at some point. It wouldn't usually be for long, and the power company will work like hell to get us up and running again."

Which again was honest, but not really what anyone wanted to hear.

After the meal, they headed once more for the library. Ellery's friends seemed to have decided the library was the heart of the house, which was funny given that Ellery and Jack rarely used that particular room. They typically gravitated toward the front drawing room with its many windows and beautiful views, especially at sunset. Now Ellery congratulated himself on having the foresight to splurge on the long leather couches and wide comfortable chairs because, with its large fireplace and enough seating, the library made a very cozy hangout.

Flip brought up their "investigation" into the Dourdos Aquamarine and Edwin Dolph.

Jack heard him out gravely. He glanced at Ellery and smiled wryly. "Proof that you're a carrier."

"Me?"

"You."

"Yeah, but does it make sense from the standpoint of a professional investigator?" Flip persisted.

"Does what make sense?" Jack asked cautiously.

"Do you think the aquamarine is what brought Dolph back to the island?"

Jack seemed to weigh the question. "You know we're not dealing with a rational intellect, right?"

"Right, of course." Ellery's friends nodded to each other like this was typical of ALL their cases.

"It makes as much sense as anything," was Jack's final, if unsatisfying, verdict. Seeing he had disappointed his audience, he added, "I can't think of another explanation for his decision to sail out here. He'd have a much better chance of evading capture on the mainland. It was a dangerous trip, given the weather conditions, and even if he managed to survive it, the island terrain isn't hospitable this time of year. If he's out there, he's not enjoying himself."

Ellery said, "If he did survive the trip, he'd probably try to make it to the tunnels beneath Pirate's Cove. That's Nora's best guess as to where Cyril Dolph would have hidden the pendant."

"The tunnels." Jack thought that over. "It makes sense for him to try. The tunnels would provide shelter and, if he knows much about the island, he knows there are emergency supplies stored there." Jack glanced at Ellery. "But the tunnels are harder to get into now."

After the events of July, new locks and other security measures had been installed to discourage trespassers in the tunnels once used for smuggling by the not-always-law-abiding citizens of Pirate's Cove. These efforts had not gone unchallenged and were still a source of contention, since most islanders considered the tunnels public property. Which they were, of course.

And, given the fact that a number of the oldest buildings had "secret" passages, long-used shortcuts, leading into the tunnels beneath the village, it was understandable not everyone was enthused by Jack's precautions.

Oscar, who had been idly glancing through Tosh's box of photos, suddenly grinned and leaned over to show Freddie a snapshot. "Hey. Your Datsun 280ZX. That was one sweet ride."

Freddie glanced at the print and laughed. "I loved that car. But man, she guzzled gas like a newborn baby."

Tosh teased, "You're going to make an alarming parent, Freddie."

Everyone laughed, including Freddie, though his gaze held Tosh's. Her cheeks got a little pink before she glanced away.

Freddie handed the photo to Jack. "What did you drive in college, Jack?"

"A blue Ford pickup." Jack studied the picture and handed it to Ellery. "I worked part time for my dad's construction business, so it made sense."

Ellery studied the photo of Freddie in jeans and shades, the epitome of young adult cool, leaning back against the side of his notorious red Datsun 280ZX.

"This looks like junior year. Who took the pic?"

Freddie took the photo back. "Noah, maybe?" He shrugged.

Another of those odd silences followed the mention of Noah's name.

"Noah," Oscar murmured. "I haven't thought of Noah in years."

"Same," Freddie said. "That was a shame. He was a nice guy. Talented."

"I don't know," Chelsea said. "I think there's a tendency to idealize someone who passes away suddenly."

Unfortunately, the relationship between Chelsea and Tosh seemed to have strained to the point where Chelsea couldn't open her mouth without Tosh taking offense.

Tosh bridled and said, "What does *that* mean?"

"Nothing," Chelsea said defensively. "I just mean, Noah wasn't any nicer or more talented than anyone else."

"Oh, my God."

"*What*? He wasn't a saint, that's all."

Lenny said quickly, "Tosh, I don't think Chelsea meant anything. Really."

"Then why say it?"

Chelsea said to Tosh, "It's not like you were any closer to Noah than the rest of us. In fact, Flip probably knew him best, and he's not jumping down my throat."

Flip said, "Come on, are we really going to argue about who knew Noah best? Let's change the subject."

Ellery said, "It's the carbs. Nothing's worse than a girl who can't handle her carbs. No more pizza nights if the ladies are going to start brawling."

Three sets of Kubrick stares swiveled his way. Three sets of Kubrick stares locked sights.

"Living dangerously, Page," Lenny observed.

"Seriously?" Chelsea said.

Tosh said nothing, though the scorching look said everything. Ellery urged, "Come on, baby. Shake it off."

Tosh made a face.

Flip said, "Kids, kids. I thought we were going to play Charades?"

This suggestion was met with approval that was probably at least fifty percent relief at the change of subject.

"Oh, God," Jack murmured.

"I pick Chels for my team," Freddie said, and got an odd look from Tosh.

Chelsea, however, flushed with happiness and forgot her earlier irritation.

"Flip," Lenny said.

"Don't keep me in suspense," Jack told Ellery, and Ellery laughed.

"I don't know. Are you any good at Charades?"

"Try me."

Ellery laughed again. "We play the movie version."

"Try me."

"I guess it's you and me, babe," Oscar told Tosh.

Tosh spluttered at the "babe" comment, but smiled reluctantly.

And, surprisingly, they all did seem to relax and have fun playing Charades.

Flip and Lenny won easily, which was just like old times, but Ellery and Jack made a decent showing. Jack turned out to be pretty good at guessing movie titles. Not so good at acting them out, but he did loosen up and seemed to enjoy himself. Chelsea and Freddie made a formidable team, while Tosh and Oscar were unexpectedly out of sync with each other, yet somehow seemed to find that hysterically funny.

When the game finally ended, it was after midnight, glasses were empty, the fire in the grate was dying, and everyone was yawning widely.

Oscar was fingering his lucky gold piece, absently sliding the coin through his fingers, flipping it across his knuckles with dexterous ease. The coin flashed in the firelight as Oscar's long fingers alternately curled and straightened, creating a continuous, almost hypnotic cycle.

Ellery remembered that nervous habit from old, but he had never really paid attention to the coin. "Is that a doubloon?"

Oscar chuckled. "Yes, but it's not an antique. I had it appraised once. It was only worth about seventy bucks."

"Oh, you do still have that?" Lenny commented. "I thought you'd lost it."

Oscar smiled at Freddie. "No. Thanks to Freddie."

Freddie looked uncomfortable. "Not really. I just picked it up off the grass and gave it back to you."

"I thought somebody might have lifted it," Flip remarked. "There was a lot of that going on back then."

There were murmurs of acknowledgement. Their dorm had been plagued with a rash of thefts their sophomore year. Ellery had lost fifty dollars. Flip had lost twenty. Freddie had lost sixty. Which was one reason they'd chosen to move off campus.

"Nope," Oscar said.

"Can I see the coin?" Ellery asked.

Oscar flipped the coin to him. Ellery caught it and examined it, showing it to Jack. It was a Spanish doubloon, though, as Oscar had said, a repro.

"Nice." Ellery flipped the coin back to Oscar, who pocketed it.

"I've really missed this," Tosh sighed.

Flip said, "Same."

"We should make it a regular thing," Lenny said.

"I would love that," Ellery said. "I'd love you to meet Dylan Carter. He runs our local theater group, the Scallywags. He was supposed to be our bartender tomorrow, but..."

"We could do an annual summer reunion!" That was Tosh.

"Leave it to the professional event coordinator," Flip teased.

"I know, but really!"

"But really, I think it's a great idea." Even as the words left Ellery's mouth, he remembered there was no longer just himself to consider. He glanced at Jack. Jack smiled at him, said to Tosh, "Sure. You should come in the summer. The weather is great and there are a lot more entertainment options."

"Then it's a plan!" Tosh clapped her hands together.

CHAPTER TWELVE

"**I**'m pretty sure Chelsea took the hatchet," Ellery said when he and Jack were upstairs undressing for bed.

"Chelsea? Why?" Though Jack didn't sound particularly surprised at this deduction.

"Well, it couldn't have been Oscar or Freddie because they didn't go outside after we arrived from the ferry. At least, not until much later. After I'd discovered the hatchet was missing. So that leaves Tosh, Flip, Lenny, and Chelsea."

"Right. But why Chelsea?"

"Methinks the lady doth protest too much?"

Jack's brows rose. "Methinks that's an interesting observation."

"Her practical jokes were always the most extreme. And, given the circumstances, there's an extreme element to this, don't you think?"

Jack nodded thoughtfully. "Given that we don't have actual proof that Dolph isn't roaming the countryside, yes."

"It's not Tosh's style. In fact, Tosh wasn't all that into the practical jokes. She'd play along, but I don't really remember her as an initiator. And I think Flip and Lenny believe Chelsea was behind it."

"Well, you'll know for sure if you find the hatchet under the mattress of Chelsea's bed after they leave."

"Speaking of which, are we for sure getting snowed in?"

Jack grimaced, glanced at the window where glimmering snow continued to fall as heavily as the special effects of a community theater stage crew. "It's looking like it. I think you're going to have to make some phone calls tomorrow morning. Even if the snow stops tonight, I don't like the idea of people trying to drive in these conditions after they've been drinking."

Ellery nodded. He'd already accepted that the house-warming party would have to be indefinitely postponed.

Jack added with a hint of apology, "It's also looking like I'll probably be staying over in Pirate's Cove tomorrow night."

Ellery opened his mouth, but closed it. He sighed. "Right. I know. There are bound to be all kinds of emergencies to deal with, great and small."

"That's the truth. Stranded vehicles, burst pipes, power outages, traffic accidents. The medical center is a concern. So is Sunset Shores. They both have backup generators, but..."

"If worse comes to worse, you'll figure something out. I have zero doubt."

Jack moved to him, folded Ellery in his arms. He kissed the bridge of Ellery's nose. "You're a very good cop's boy-friend—fiancé. Have I told you that lately?"

"I like hearing it," Ellery admitted.

It was nice standing there in each other's arms.

Nice in the obvious way of warm bare skin and shared heartbeats. But also nice in knowing with certainty that Jack was always going to do his best to be there for him. Ellery had loved both Brandon and Todd, but it hadn't been anything close to his feelings for Jack. A huge part of that was because of the kind of person Jack was—and the kind of love that Jack offered.

He was the strongest guy Ellery knew, but he was also the kindest. He was honest and reliable and he sincerely cared about people. He was always going to try to do his best, because that's who he was.

There were probably people who wouldn't find those qualities, that kind of caring, quite as alluring as Ellery did. But after Brandon and Todd, Ellery had learned to value someone who told the truth and habitually put the needs of others before himself.

"What's the mystery surrounding Noah?" Jack asked suddenly, interrupting Ellery's peaceful thoughts.

"There really isn't a mystery." Ellery felt that familiar sadness. "Noah was killed in a hit-and-run during our junior year at Tisch."

"So, your friend Noah was killed in a hit-and-run, and your character in the *Happy Halloween* movies is named Noah *Street*?"

"I know," Ellery said glumly. "Dark. But I didn't name him. Brandon did. He considered it an homage to Noah." He added, "But in Brandon's defense, Noah's death was a traumatic event in our lives. It had a big effect on all of us."

When he didn't continue, Jack asked, "Was the driver caught?"

"No." Ellery added, "There were no witnesses. It happened late at night."

"Where did it happen?"

"A few streets from the apartment we were renting after we all moved from Third Avenue North. Noah was walking back from Tisch. He had a night class."

"We being...?"

"Flip, Noah, Brandon—off and on—and I were sharing an apartment in Manhattan. Not far from where Tosh and Freddie were living. Chelsea and Lenny briefly moved in together; they were in Greenpoint. Oscar was living on his own, but after Noah died, he moved in with Flip and me."

Jack asked, "No security cameras?"

"There was footage from one camera, but it was so dark and grainy, you couldn't even make out the model of car, let alone the color. The only other camera with a view of the street had been damaged in an electrical storm the day before."

Jack grunted. "That's bad luck."

"The worst," Ellery agreed.

After a moment, Jack asked, "Did anyone in your group have a beef with Noah? Were there any issues there?"

"A *beef*?" Ellery echoed. He drew back, stared at Jack in alarm. "Noah's death was an accident. There was never any doubt about that. Nobody had any problems with Noah."

Even as he said it, he recognized the irony. He was the one usually seeing mysteries everywhere, often to Jack's frustration. Now he was reacting like everyone else usually did when he started speculating.

"Would everyone agree with that?" Jack asked.

"Yes. I'm certain of it. Noah was one of the nicest people I ever met. Super easygoing. I don't think he ever squabbled with anyone." Ellery added quickly, "Also, he did jaywalk everywhere. All the time. He's the only person I ever met who actually managed to get ticketed for jaywalking. So, he..."

To Ellery's astonishment—and alarm—Jack smoothed his hand up and down his back, in an absently soothing gesture, as if he understood how upsetting this was.

But it shouldn't be upsetting. Because it really *had* been an accident. No one had ever questioned that.

Ellery said firmly, "No, but really, Jack. What started you thinking—" he swallowed on the rest of it in a little distressed gulp.

Jack reassured, "I don't have any reason to suspect anything. But I can't help noticing that any time Noah's name comes up, there's always tension, always a pause, like none of you know what to say."

"Well, because it's painful. It was a huge shock to all of us. Honestly, it's one of the most shocking things that ever happened to me." Ellery amended, "I mean, until I moved here and started stumbling over bodies left and right."

Jack grimaced in acknowledgement.

"And I know that's true of all of us."

"Of course it was. You were all very young."

Granted, Jack was only a few years older and at that time would probably have been starting his police training.

And, as much as he hated to admit it, Ellery too had noticed that uncomfortable undercurrent when Noah's name came up. It was almost as if they were all waiting for the other shoe to drop.

But there had never been another shoe!

Or, rather, there had never been any reason to believe that Noah's accident had been anything but that. The police had asked questions, naturally, but it had all been informal and cursory. The case was closed in a day, the conclusion foregone: Noah Tandy had died in a tragic accident.

The kind of thing that happened all too often.

"Was alcohol involved?"

"No. He was at class, Jack. He wasn't coming home from the pub!"

But Jack, following his own thoughts, said, "Chelsea said Flip and Noah were especially close?"

Ellery felt another of those unwarranted flashes of concern. "Yes. They shared a room when we all still lived on campus that first couple of years."

"Was Noah gay?"

"No. No way."

"Was Flip interested in Noah?"

Ellery didn't want to answer. Not because he thought Flip had anything to do with Noah's death. But he knew how Jack thought. How Jack interpreted things. Jack hunted for recognizable patterns. And once he found a pattern, he searched for the inevitable loose threads. And once he found a loose thread, he started pulling. He pulled and kept pulling until everything unraveled and he had his suspect in custody.

"Yes. At first. But as soon as Noah made it clear he wasn't interested in anything but friendship, that was it. Flip accepted it and moved on. They were close. Really." Ellery added, "By the way, Flip didn't own a car. None of us did except Freddie."

"Did Flip ever borrow Freddie's car?"

Ellery was starting to get exasperated. "We *all* borrowed Freddie's car. Freddie was always generous about that kind of thing."

Jack's mouth curved ruefully. "Sorry. This is bothering you more than I expected."

Why *was* it bothering him so much?

Because Jack had unerringly managed to tap into a tiny vein of subconscious disquiet?

"It's not logical," Ellery agreed. "But it's hard thinking that one of us, one of our group, could have had anything to do with it." He added, probably tellingly, "If one of us *was* somehow involved, it would have been an accident."

Jack nodded, but that was in acknowledgement not necessarily agreement. He said, "How did Freddie and N—"

"Oh my God, Jack!"

Jack gave a sheepish laugh. "Sorry. Habits of the trade."

Ellery shook his head, but said, "I would say Noah and Freddie probably had the least interaction. Like me and Chelsea. We didn't have a lot in common then, and I don't think we have *anything* in common now except a shared circle of friends. Freddie and Noah didn't have classes together, didn't share rooms, and in my opinion, didn't interact enough to have any conflict."

Jack nodded, met Ellery's eyes. His blue-green gaze softened. "I'm sorry if this has opened old wounds."

"No," Ellery said. "You're right. We do all get quiet and... strained when Noah's name comes up. I've always figured it's because it was a traumatic event and it's still unresolved. But maybe there's something else there. Survivor's guilt or something."

Jack murmured something gentle and noncommittal. He kissed Ellery. Ellery kissed Jack.

Outside the window, the snow continued to tumble in big white flakes, like flannel cut-out stars falling from a felt board sky.

Snow slowly, silently building up on the window sills.

"What are the chances they're all staying in their own beds tonight?" Jack inquired lazily, a while later.

By then they were in the small-galleon-sized bed, tucked between the flannel sheets, warm and comfortably relaxed in the nest of blankets and pillows. Ellery's head was cushioned on Jack's broad shoulder. Jack's hand lightly threaded Ellery's hair.

Ellery chuckled. "Little to none, I'd say. I just hope Watson doesn't start barking when the first floorboard creaks."

Watson, curled in a black ball at the foot of the bed, opened one eye, considered them, closed his eye.

Jack's laugh sounded slightly evil. "I wouldn't bet on that."

They both grinned at Watson.

"Who do you think will end up where?" Jack sounded thoughtful.

Ellery considered. "I think Tosh will end up with Oscar."

"Yep," Jack agreed. "That would be my guess."

Ellery mused, "I think Chelsea will try for Freddie, but I'm not sure how that's going to go over."

"*Ah.* I was going to say," Jack commented. "It's not my imagination, right?"

"No."

"She's deliberately trying to look like Tosh?"

That wasn't quite what Ellery expected to hear, but Jack was right about that. "It kind of looks that way."

"Because Chelsea looks nothing like she did in those college photos."

Ellery made a face. "In the interests of fairness..."

Jack chuckled, tugged gently on Ellery's forelock. "You were pretty skinny, yeah, and the hair almost counted as another person, but other than that, you look mostly the same. Same taste in jeans and T-shirts. I think you're still wearing the same pair of tennis shoes you had on in that photo with Noah."

"I grew into my nose."

Jack leaned over and nuzzled the nose in question. "It's a very nice nose, I must say."

Ellery smiled beneath these attentions; paid them back in kind.

"But yeah," Ellery returned to their earlier conversation. "Aggressive mimicry."

"Hmm?"

"It's when predators or parasites mimic harmless species to get closer to their prey. Chelsea's even wearing her hair like Tosh now."

For some reason Jack seemed to find that funny.

"What? It's a Trivial Pursuit question," Ellery protested.

"I believe you. And you think the transformation is all on Freddie's behalf?"

"Maybe not entirely. Chelsea's ambitious. She's talking about moving out to Hollywood. She has to know if she's going to make it on the West coast, she has to look the part. No pun intended. Tosh is the obvious role model."

Jack stopped laughing. "Now, between *those* two, there's enough friction to start a campfire."

"I think that might be where Freddie comes in because Freddie—"

"Still has feelings for Tosh," Jack agreed.

Ellery moved his head in assent. "You're very observant." Not that it came as a surprise. In fact, sometimes he wished Jack wasn't *quite* so observant.

"It's part of the job." Which was true.

Ellery said, "But Freddie does like Chelsea. They were pals in college. They stayed close even after Freddie and Tosh split. Granted, Freddie and Tosh weren't asking people to take sides. It was a pretty civilized split."

"Nice when it happens. Which isn't often enough."

"Tosh is still fond of Freddie. And vice versa."

"Sure," Jack said. "But I'm guessing the feelings run deeper for Freddie."

"Yes. But he approves of Chelsea's makeover, that's for sure. So maybe she'll finally get her wish."

Jack's mouth curved. "Maybe. Unfortunately, friendship doesn't always turn to love."

"Not always," Ellery smiled ruefully, recalling a rather painful period in their own friendship.

Jack said softly, "But it's sure nice when it does," and leaned over to kiss Ellery.

It was some time later when a floorboard creaked along the hallway.

Eyes closed, Ellery listened to that cautious squeak, step, squeak. He smiled and went back to sleep.

CHAPTER THIRTEEN

Ellery woke on Saturday morning to a world blanketed in white silence.

Actually, it was more like a world smothered by white silence because everything, as far as the eye could see, was a formless ghost of its normal shape.

The good news was, the snow fall had slowed. The bad news was, it had not completely stopped, and delicate snow-flakes continued to drift down from the heavy skies.

Jack had left at some point in the pre-dawn hours. Ellery had a vague memory of a kiss and a promise to phone later. More than anything he wanted to go back to bed and sleep for a few more hours. As much as he was enjoying having his friends visit, it was tiring playing host for days on end. Even with everyone pitching in, he was doing more cooking, cleaning, and fixing cocktails—not to mention drinking cocktails—than he'd done in a year.

He closed his eyes. The house was very quiet, everyone still asleep. He listened to the snow gently brushing the windows...the slow sonorous chimes of the grandfather clock downstairs...(eight o'clock, still plenty early)...the eager panting in his ear...

Ellery's eyes popped open.

Watson gazed hopefully down at him.

Ellery moaned, "Just this once can't we sleep in?"

This un-Ellery-like sentiment was clearly cause for concern, and Watson commenced the verification process with much snuffling and sniffing, ignoring Ellery's laughing protests.

Identification complete, Watson sneezed noisily in Ellery's face and jumped off the bed. He proceeded to jump up and down, in rhythmic heavy thuds—Ellery could have sworn he was deliberately planting all his weight on the landings.

"*Shhhh*!" Ellery hissed. "You're going to wake everyone up."

Up.

DOWN.

Up.

DOWN.

The steady thump could have doubled for the sound effects of a tympanon drum setting the pace for the crew manning the oars of a Roman galley.

Ellery swore softly, threw back the covers, and staggered into the bathroom. He winced at his reflection—talk about hair!—brushed his teeth, and exited to search for something clean to wear.

A few minutes later, suitably bundled against the elements, he followed the herd of elephants, AKA Watson, down the stairs and out the front door.

The sharp, cold air made him gasp, but it effectively dispelled the last cobwebs of sleep. There was snow right up to the top of the front steps. How the heck much snow *was* that?

Too much. That was for sure.

Watson, both intrigued and alarmed by all that white stuff, sniffed cautiously from the edge of the steps, moved cautiously forward, and sank into the snow.

He hopped out again, shook himself mightily, and looked at Ellery for guidance.

Ellery stopped laughing and gave him a quick pat. "You're okay. You're going to get a good workout running through this stuff." He left the steps, sinking down to his shins into soft white powder. "Come on, pal."

Still dubious, Watson followed. As suspected, it didn't take long for him to realize that snow was pretty fun stuff, especially when your best friend was nearby to pull you out of the deep drifts.

When Watson had tired of running through snow, biting snow, barking at snow, and jumping in snow, Ellery whistled for him and they returned to the house.

Tosh, in a black kimono-style dressing gown, was making coffee in the kitchen. Two prepped mugs sat on the counter.

She started guiltily as Ellery and Watson entered, Watson shaking his coat repeatedly and noisily. "Oops. I thought I was the only one up. Okay if I take these upstairs?"

"Of course." Ellery hunted for a towel to dry off Watson. He couldn't help teasing, "Sleep okay?"

Tosh laughed, staring at the coffee perking in the machine. Then she looked up, said earnestly, "I really like Jack."

Ellery, kneeling beside Watson, replied, "Me, too."

"I wasn't sure at first because he seems so...so..."

"Serious?" Ellery suggested wryly.

"Well, yeah. But I think he's serious in a good way. He's...authentic."

Ellery had never particularly thought about it, but yeah, if by *authentic* she meant Jack was honest and unpretentious, then Jack was authentic.

Watson rewarded his efforts with a quick kiss. Ellery rose and opened the fridge to get Watson's food out.

Tosh said, "I mean, *reliable* may not sound sexy, but when you've been with someone who *isn't* reliable…"

Ellery wasn't sure if Tosh meant Freddie because Freddie had been a long time ago and Tosh had dated plenty since. In fact, Tosh probably *didn't* mean Freddie. She probably meant Brandon or Todd. And there she had nailed it.

Besides, reliable or not, Jack was totally sexy. Reliability was just icing on the cake.

He finished preparing Watson's food, set the metal bowl on the floor, and Watson proceeded to give a stirring portrayal of a pup who hadn't eaten in months.

Tosh poured the coffee into the mugs. "But also, it's pretty clear that whatever you want is fine with Jack."

"Wellll, I wouldn't go *that* far," Ellery had plenty of experience with Jack expressing his feelings when he *wasn't* fine with what Ellery wanted.

Tosh finished doctoring the coffee and picked up the mugs. "Anyway, *this* one is a keeper."

"I'm going to do my best."

They exchanged grins, and Tosh started upstairs, Watson, having already gulped down his breakfast, following.

Ellery spent a couple of minutes deciding what to feed the human members of the house party, eventually deciding on bacon and gruyere egg bites, fruit, and pastries. While the bacon cooked, he began phoning the people he'd invited to the housewarming to let them know the party was off.

There was a flattering consensus of expressed disappointment, but no real surprise.

Nora said, "It's the right decision, dearie. Especially with more snow on the way."

"*Is* there more snow on the way?" Unhappily, Ellery glanced out the kitchen windows.

"According to popular opinion."

"Or unpopular opinion."

Nora said bracingly, "It's always fun to share adventures with good friends. Next time you get together you'll be able to reminisce about the time you were snowed in at an isolated country house with an axe murderer on the loose."

Ellery only heard one part of that sentence. "Is there reason to think Edwin Dolph is still on the loose?"

"No, no. But we can't be sure that he *isn't.*"

She sounded unreasonably upbeat about it.

Ellery phoned Dylan next.

"I figured that was coming," Dylan said. "But if you have to be snowed in, these are probably the best possible circumstances."

"True. Other than the possibility of an axe murderer roaming the countryside."

Dylan scoffed at the idea. "I'm sure Dolph is at the bottom of the deep blue sea, even as we speak." He added alarmingly, "*However...*"

Ellery frowned. "However, what?"

"Cyrus is out on bail."

"*What?*"

Dylan added wryly, "And planning to run for office again."

"Cyrus is going to run for mayor? He's been charged with multiple murders!"

"I know. Jack is fit to be tied."

"But I thought he couldn't get bail?"

"It seems that some of his old connections are still...connected."

Ellery protested, "He tried to kill me!"

"He wouldn't have any reason to try again."

Did Dylan think that was reassuring?

"B-b-but..."

"Oh, I agree," Dylan assured. "I don't *think* he'll be re-elected."

Ellery's final phone call was to Sue Lewis, editor and owner of the *Scuttlebutt Weekly*. Given their contentious history, Ellery had struggled with himself over inviting Sue. But they had recently called a truce, and not inviting her would have seemed pointed. Plus, Jack had felt it was the smart and diplomatic thing to do.

"I knew this was coming," Sue informed him. "But since you're all snowed in out there with nothing to do, do you think it's possible I might be able to get a phone interview with Fredrick Ames?"

It was astonishing to think anyone managed to keep *any* secrets in this village. But of course, Freddie was a bona fide celebrity, so his arrival on Buck Island would not go unnoticed. Especially since he'd been signing autographs on the dock.

"I can ask," Ellery said. "I'll give him your cell number and if he's interested, he can phone you."

"I could phone him directly if—"

"Mmm. No." Ellery said, "I promise I'll give him your number."

Lenny and Flip appeared as he was hanging up. Flip sniffed the air.

"Bacon and coffee. You had me at bacon."

"I'll take coffee. How can you possibly be hungry after last night?" Lenny said.

Flip shrugged, glanced around the kitchen as though expecting to see people hiding beneath the table, "Where is everybody?"

"It's perfect weather for sleeping in," Ellery said.

"It's perfect weather for something," Lenny murmured.

Flip snickered. "Yeah, it sounded like people were playing musical beds last night." He added, "Where's Watson?"

"Upstairs with Tosh and—Tosh."

Lenny rolled her eyes, and wandered over to the stove. "Is it okay if I make tea?"

"You don't have to ask."

Lenny filled the tea kettle, gazing out the window. "Wow, that's a lot of snow."

Ellery said, "How did I miss Tosh and Oscar? I thought it was always Belle and Oscar."

"Oh, it was," Lenny got a couple of mugs from the cupboard. "But eventually that fizzled out. There was always a little spark between Tosh and Oscar."

"*Was* there?"

Lenny and Flip laughed at him. Lenny, coffee pot in hand, said, "You need a top up, Ell?"

"Nope. I'm good."

"Oh my gosh. Are those *croissants* in the oven?"

Ellery said, "Chocolate croissants, yeah."

"You are the greatest host ever."

"It's not like I did anything but defrost them."

"I don't know how I'm going to be able to return to real life after this." Lenny carried a mug of coffee to the table and sat down with Ellery and Flip.

For a few contented moments there was only the sound of the tea kettle hissing and the trees creaking beneath snow.

Then Flip said, "You know Chelsea took that hatchet, right?"

"Did you see her take it?"

"No. But it's totally on brand."

Ellery agreed but stayed noncommittal.

Lenny said, "If we find Tosh with a hatchet in her back, we'll know who did it."

"Yikes," Ellery said. "That went dark fast."

Lenny shrugged. "Chels is jealous of Tosh. She always has been, but in college it was different. Having Tosh to hang around with worked to her benefit. Plus, she was always smugly aware she was more talented."

"Except she didn't get the roles," Flip said. "Anytime she and Tosh went up against each other, Tosh won."

"And Tosh is winning now," Lenny said grimly. "When it comes to Freddie."

Neither Ellery nor Flip had anything to say to that.

"Did Jack get off okay?" Flip asked suddenly.

"Huh?" Ellery stared at him blankly and both Flip and Lenny started laughing.

Lenny said, "Look, he still blushes. That's adorbs."

Ellery said, "Could you two please make yourselves useful somehow?"

"Yep, what can we do?" Flip said briskly.

"I don't know. Help me figure out lunch."

"Lunch?" Flip and Lenny looked at each other in alarm.

"Dinner," Ellery corrected with a glance at the clock. It seemed that most of their crew had the same impulse he'd had that morning. And Watson, the little scoundrel, was enjoying a lie-in with them.

Lenny was musing, "That was so fun last night. Who would have dreamed Jack would be good at Charades?"

"Not me," Ellery admitted.

"Maybe he used to do a lot of undercover work for LAPD?"

Flip started to laugh. "As what? A mime?"

The tea kettle began to whistle.

Lenny made a face at Flip and went to pour her tea.

When she returned to the table, Ellery said slowly, "This is going to come out of left field, I know, but did either of you ever think maybe Noah's accident wasn't an accident?"

Lenny and Flip stared at him.

"What do you mean?" Flip asked.

Lenny said, "You mean someone ran him down on purpose?"

Hearing it put so succinctly was disturbing.

Ellery shook his head. "I don't know what I mean."

No one said a word. The tick-tock of the kitchen clock sounded ominously loud in the abrupt silence.

Flip's lips parted and Lenny said quickly, "No."

Flip looked at her. "Len."

Lenny shook her head. "*No.* We agreed. And dredging this up *now* really makes no sense. None."

Flip's look to Ellery was apologetic.

"Wait a minute," Ellery said. "You mean, you *did* think at the time that there was something wrong?"

"Not at the time," Flip said.

"Well, of course there was something wrong. It was a hit-and-run," Lenny said.

"Right but... That's someone running away from an *accident.*"

Flip asked, "Is it? Was it?"

"*Wasn't* it?"

"Of course, it was." Lenny scowled at Flip.

Flip, busy scowling at Ellery, didn't notice.

"But why wouldn't it have been an accident?" Ellery objected. "What would be the reason for wanting Noah... gone."

"There isn't one." Flip shook his head. "Noah was as nice a guy as they came."

"Then..."

Once again no one seemed to know what to say.

Finally, Lenny glanced at the open doorway and said quietly, "Accidents happen. But that one just seemed...off. Wrong."

"It *was* wrong," Ellery said. "It should never have happened. That doesn't mean..." He hesitated to put it into words, especially since neither Lenny nor Flip had. He said finally, keeping his voice as low as Lenny's, "It doesn't mean it had anything to do with any of *us*."

"Agreed," Lenny said quickly. "Exactly."

"So why are we whispering?"

Flip pressed his lips together.

Lenny said shortly, "Because it's a sensitive subject."

True. But as far as Ellery could tell, Lenny and Flip shared his unease over Noah's death, though, like himself, had nothing to base it on. Why assume they were the only ones who felt this way?

Or did Flip know more than he was saying? It was hard to tell. If so, he wasn't going to share it with Lenny around. Lenny was adamantly opposed to ripping open old wounds, and maybe that was the most sensible attitude.

A floorboard squeaked in the hall. Ellery, Flip, and Lenny stared in silence.

Over a minute later, Chelsea appeared in the kitchen doorway. Her hair was piled into a messy bun, and she wore a heavy vintage style men's Beacon bathrobe—and last night's eye makeup.

"Where is everybody?" she asked, slumping into a chair at the kitchen table.

Since the people now present made up more than half of *everybody*, it was perhaps not the most tactful comment.

Ellery said, "I think everyone's having a lazy day."

"How nice," Chelsea said bitterly. "Could we even get out the front door if we needed to?"

"Yep. The snow's up to the top of the steps, but we can get out. I'm just not sure why we would need to. Or where we would go. We can't drive anywhere."

She groaned. "So, we really *are* stuck here until God knows when? *Great.*"

Flip said dryly, "I'm sure Ellery feels the same."

Chelsea made a face. "Ellery knows what I mean."

"I don't doubt that."

Chelsea looked to Ellery for understanding. "It's just that *we* all have lives to get back to."

Lenny looked at her in disbelief. "Maybe stop now, Chels."

"My God everyone is so *touchy* this morning." Chelsea rested her forehead on her fists. "Ellery, do you have anything for a headache?"

"Sure. Aspirin or ibuprofen?"

"Both. And an ice pack, if you have it."

Ellery winked at Lenny and Flip and went to get Chelsea painkillers and ice.

When he'd handed over the medical supplies, Chelsea tottered out of the kitchen and returned upstairs.

Flip shook his head. "I don't know about Chelsea, but a day of nothing to do but eat, drink, and relax sounds like heaven to me. I haven't had a vacation like this in years."

"Same." Lenny added, "You know she was standing outside the kitchen listening to us, right?"

Ellery nodded. He had unconsciously timed Chelsea's entrance from the point the floorboard squeaked to when she stepped into the doorway.

"She's been doing that all weekend," Flip commented. "I'm not sure what she thinks she's going to hear."

"Nothing good," Lenny retorted.

CHAPTER FOURTEEN

The hall clock was chiming eleven o'clock when Tosh and Oscar appeared, Watson in tow. They were carrying their coffee mugs. Tosh had dressed in jeans and a man's oversized flannel shirt. Oscar was in jeans and a green wool sweater. They had a distinct honeymoon glow about them.

"Morning! It is *gorgeous* out," Tosh exclaimed. "Freddie's talking about organizing a snowball fight."

"Since when are snowball fights organized?" Ellery *oofed* as Watson leaped onto his lap and made himself at home. He gazed severely into Watson's big brown eyes. "Just wait till they find out how much you eat."

Tosh was checking out the breakfast options and murmuring approval. Oscar helped himself to coffee.

"More coffee, Tosh?" he asked.

"Not for me."

Tosh sat down across from Ellery, folding her arms on the table surface. "So, here's a weird thing. I can't find my photos anywhere."

Ellery did a doubletake. "That can't...are you sure?"

Tosh nodded. Her smile was rueful. "I remembered them when we were—after we went up. And I remembered what Flip said, and I thought maybe I ought to—"

"What did Flip say?" Ellery interrupted.

"Well, actually, he didn't say anything."

Ellery blinked.

"What I mean is, he reminded me to take the box with me when I was going up to bed, and afterwards I felt like maybe there had been something pointed about it."

Ellery had known Tosh a long time, but even so, it took him a few seconds to work that out. "You mean, you think Flip was warning you that someone...it would have to be Chelsea he meant, right? That Chelsea was liable to take your photos?"

Tosh sat back. "Okay. It sounds ridiculous when you say it aloud."

"Is it possible you set the box somewhere for safe keeping?"

Tosh shook her head. "No. I left it on the wooden trunk between the sofas. I remember that. You and Jack were still looking at the photos."

Ellery thought back. "That's right. And we were the last two to go up."

Oscar joined them at the table, his expression serious. "I came down with Tosh to help her look. The box wasn't there. It's still not."

"Okay, but why would someone steal your photos? What I mean is, we've all been looking at those photos for two days. I didn't notice anything incriminating or—"

"No," Tosh said quickly. "I don't mean anything like *that*. They're just old college photos. No, I was thinking—well, actually, Oscar thinks Chelsea might just want the photos."

"Want them for what?"

"For herself."

At Ellery's look of noncomprehension, Oscar said, "Because of Freddie."

"Oh. Okay, I'm still not quite..."

Tosh said, "Because she couldn't just take the photos of Freddie, right?"

"Right."

"She'd have to take the whole box or it would be obvious who took them. And why."

"Yes," Ellery said firmly, though his tone was more like *huh?*

Tosh sighed, turned to Oscar. "It does sound crazy."

"No, it doesn't," Oscar assured her. To Ellery, he said, "Ell, you have to have noticed Chelsea is obsessed with Freddie."

"I know she always liked Freddie." Ellery hesitated to use the word *obsessed*. Partly because it was such a loaded word, but partly because he had never really paid enough attention to Chelsea to know if she was obsessed with Freddie or not.

"She always had a thing about Freddie," Tosh said. "But I didn't think about it because we always joked about it."

"Who? You and Freddie?"

"No. Me and Chelsea. She used to joke about stealing Freddie from me, but I didn't take it seriously because she *was* joking about it, making fun of herself. But also, because it's ridiculous for grown-ups to talk about stealing people from other people."

"Sure." It was also ridiculous for grown-ups to steal photos of their crushes, from their friends.

"I assumed she'd outgrown it. We've all moved on from those original— But then when we met up at Point Judith and she was dressed like...like..."

"Your mini-me," Oscar supplied.

"Well, yes. Honestly? This is going to sound terrible, but I actually wondered if she'd been stalking me."

Ellery said uncomfortably, "I did notice her taste in clothes had changed."

None of this made sense to him. Why would Chelsea start stalking Tosh after all this time? And to what purpose? To get fashion tips? Yeesh.

Tosh said, "It's a lot more than her taste in clothes. It's increasingly obvious to me that she's *still* infatuated with Freddie."

"The mystery is, why he's encouraging her," Oscar said grimly.

Ellery and Tosh briefly met eyes. Tosh said, "I don't want to make things awkward, especially for you, Ell. But I want my photos back. They have a lot of sentimental value for me."

"Of course, they do," Ellery said quickly. "Of course, you want them back. What would you like me to do? Do you want me to talk to Chelsea?"

He couldn't think of anything he *less* wanted to do.

"No. How fair would that be?" Tosh said. "No, I can talk to her. It's just, I know Chelsea. I know there's going to be a giant scene, no matter how I try to approach the subject. I don't know that there *is* a tactful way to approach this. And I don't want to ruin the weekend for everyone."

"No. Right," Ellery said absently. He was thinking about the logistics of Chelsea taking—and keeping—a box that size in a house that was not her own.

"But..."

Ellery said again, "Right."

Tosh said, "I could wait until we're closer to leaving?"

Oscar said, "Maybe? That way if she has a meltdown..."

"Actually, I have an idea." Ellery put Watson on the floor and rose. "Do you know if Chelsea's up yet?"

"I didn't hear her moving around." Oscar said, as Tosh pushed her chair back.

"Good." Ellery headed for the library, Tosh and Oscar and Watson on his heels.

When they entered the library, Ellery went straight to the bookshelves at the far end of the room. He reached the hidden door leading to the secret passage and pushed the door, triggering the spring latch. A gust of damp, dark air floated from deep inside the tunnel.

Oscar whistled. "*Very* cool."

"Right?" Tosh said. "Ellery says the house is riddled with secret passages."

Ellery stepped inside the passage, saying over his shoulder, "Don't block the doorway, I need the light."

He was wishing he'd thought to grab a flashlight, but he didn't have to go more than a few steps before he spotted the blue box safely wedged between two joists nailed to open wall studs in the wall of the tunnel.

"Found them," he called.

"You *did*?" Tosh squeaked.

Ellery lifted the box from its hiding place and walked back to the entrance. He handed the box to Tosh.

"I don't think you have to say anything to her."

"Oh, *Ellery*. Thank you." Tosh clutched the box, then hesitated and held it back out to him. "Maybe you should keep them until we're ready to leave."

"I think that's a good idea," Oscar interjected. "No way is she going to risk going through *your* rooms."

Now there was a hair-raising thought. "Do you think she'd actually—"

"I wouldn't have thought she'd do *this*," Tosh was still holding the box out to Ellery. He took it reluctantly.

She said, "I'm sorry to involve you."

"Well, no. Of course, I'm involved. I'm sorry this happened to you. And, yes, this is probably the simplest solution. I'll hang onto these until you leave."

"Up until this very moment I still thought maybe it was a misunderstanding or that they had somehow been put to the side."

"It's an uncomfortable situation," Ellery agreed. That was putting it mildly. He couldn't help wishing he could talk this development over with Jack, but the last thing Jack needed was to be bothered with stuff like this. He already had his hands full with genuine emergencies.

"Hopefully, this will be the end of it," Oscar said.

"Hopefully," Tosh replied. She sounded as doubtful as Ellery felt.

Arf! Arf! Arf!

The snow-packed courtyard outside Captain's Seat was a blizzard of activity as flurries of snowballs whizzed through the air—most of them missing their targets. Laughter echoed off the trees and stone walls.

Freddie, unsurprisingly, was in his element, hurling snowballs with the precision of a quarterback. At one point, he playfully targeted Tosh, neatly knocking the toque from her head. Tosh, hair tumbled around her face, burst into laughter and retaliated, her snowballs finding their mark on Freddie's broad chest. Oscar leaped (unnecessarily, as it turned out) to her defense, his aim surprisingly good for someone more accustomed to handling reels of film than the tools of the action hero trade.

Watson—deemed off target by Ellery before the first snowball was launched—ran from ice fort to ice fort—barking excitedly in a misguided attempt to restore law and order. Jack's influence was no doubt wearing off on him.

Nobody was winning. Nobody was losing. Everyone seemed to be having a great time.

Chelsea launched an impressive barrage of ice bombs in Freddie's direction, though most of them flew wide. Freddie, grinning, egged her on, gesturing to his chest, his head, and then widely over his head. He yodeled in a falsetto, "Yo-del-Ay-Ee-Oooo!"

Chelsea's aim got even wilder.

Or maybe she did mean to paste Tosh in the face. Twice.

Nearby, Lenny and Flip worked as a team, seeming to mostly play defense, building the walls of their fort impressively high and stockpiling snowballs for the...winter? Lenny laughed crazily as Flip dramatically dove behind the fort, doing an action hero somersault as he narrowly avoided a snowball from Oscar.

As host, Ellery felt it was his duty to make sure all participants received equal attention, and he pelted snowballs at anyone within range. Watson naturally mistook Ellery's snowballs for the balls they played chase with, and darted after Ellery's missiles, barking excitedly and occasionally catching a stray snowball in his mouth—to his continued bafflement.

When Ellery's cell phone rang and Jack's photo flashed up, he called for a time-out and rose from the behind the mound of his fort. He was promptly hit by a shower of snowballs.

"That's it. I'm phoning the U.N.!" he called, and of course was hit with another volley of snowballs.

He retreated to the front steps of the mansion, answered the phone, and gulped, "Hey!"

"Hey. What's happening at the North Pole?" Jack inquired.

"We're having a snowball fight."

"Of course."

"The bad news is you couldn't get back if you wanted to."

"Well, I do want to, of course. But I'll be staying over in the village tonight. What's the good news?"

"Me and Watson are winning the snowball fight?"

Jack made a sound of amusement. "Glad to hear it. Anything else to report?"

"Watson will be crushed to learn you're not coming home tonight."

"Just Watson?"

Ellery scrubbed the snow from his eyelashes with his mittened hand. "You will be sorely missed by other household members as well."

Jack chuckled, then grew serious. "Listen, I had a little free time this morning—"

"That's hard to believe."

"You're not kidding. Especially with the way my afternoon is going. Anyway, I did some quick preliminary research on Noah Tandy's death—"

Ellery's good mood faded. "What? *Why?*"

"—and I've filed an official request for information with NYPD's Records and Identification Division."

"*Jack.* This is—this makes no sense. Why are you involving yourself in this? There's no case here. There's nothing here to investigate."

"Then there's nothing to worry about, right?"

"But this is—I don't understand what you're trying to do."

Jack said calmly, "I don't understand why you're so against this."

"Because these people are my friends. Because there's nothing to find out so there's no reason to-to open old wounds."

"I'm not opening old wounds. I'm checking into a few things to satisfy my own curiosity. No one other than you ever needs to know anything about it." Jack added grimly, "Unless, my instinct is correct and there's something not quite right about Tandy's death."

Ellery felt a chill that had nothing to do with the ice melting down the back of his neck.

"What do you think is not quite right?"

"If I knew, I wouldn't have to make an official inquiry."

Ellery protested, "But if you don't have anything to go on, I don't understand why you're making official inquiries."

Jack hesitated. "Would you say you have an instinct for knowing when something isn't right?"

Ellery said unwillingly, "You mean when I stick my nose into other people's business whether they ask for my help or not?"

"Exactly. Because, although it doesn't give me pleasure, I've had to admit that you do have a talent for solving mysteries. At the very least, you have a talent for sensing that there's a mystery to be solved."

Ellery knew exactly where this was headed. He said grudgingly, "I guess so."

"And would you then agree that I *also* have an instinct for knowing when things are not right? Call it a cop's instinct."

"Yes. Of course. We both know you're good at what you do. But we've both gotten things wrong in the past, Jack. We've both made mistakes. You were wrong about Dylan."

"I was. Yes."

"And, you know that I wasn't afraid to-to take a hard look at everything that happened."

"Exactly. You believed Dylan was innocent."

"I did. But even if he hadn't been—"

"You wanted the truth."

"Yes!"

"Do you see what I'm trying to get at?"

"*No.* You've just proved that I'm not afraid of an investigation that might involve people I care about."

"But you don't want this crime investigated?"

"*Because there's nothing there.* There's nothing to find after all this time. How would you possibly hunt down this unknown driver?"

"I think there *is* something there," Jack said. "My instinct tells me that there's something there. And I think, deep down, you—*all* of you—know it, too. Which is why none of you want to touch it with a ten-foot pole."

Ellery was silent.

"You weren't afraid to help Dylan because you believed he was innocent. But you *are* afraid for me to look into a decade-old closed case. Why? Because your instinct is telling you someone you're fond of is probably involved."

Ellery wanted to deny it, but Jack had unerringly put his finger on the problem. A problem Ellery did not want to acknowledge even existed.

He said unwillingly, "It's a long time ago, Jack."

"So, it's okay if someone killed one of your friends a long time ago."

"You know that's not what I'm saying."

Jack said quite gently, "Isn't it, though?"

"If—*if*—anyone I know had something to do with it, it would have been an accident. *That*, I'm sure of."

"Okay, well, if you're sure, don't you think it would be a relief to that person to have the truth come out? To be able to accept responsibility and clear their conscience?"

After a moment, Ellery said, "I wish you hadn't told me."

"Is that true?"

Ellery let out a long breath. "No. It's not true. But."

"I know. This is a tough one. And like you said, I've been wrong before. I could be wrong about this."

"I really think you are, Jack."

He really didn't, though. That was the problem.

Jack said, "But to be on the safe side, don't share this conversation with anyone. In fact, try to avoid the subject of Noah."

"Right," Ellery said automatically. It was a little late for that.

"Good. If someone *was* involved in Noah's death, maybe it would be a relief to have the truth come out. But they've been hiding this secret a long time. We can't be sure what they might do to make sure the truth stays buried."

CHAPTER FIFTEEN

S U B T E R F U G E

Sixteen points, according to Collins Scrabble Words. However, Ellery's friends were going by the internet site Word Unscrambler, and granted him a whopping twenty-two points. He graciously took the extra points, putting him well in the lead.

"This is why no one wants to play with you," Chelsea said from the growing distance of second place. "You always win."

"Ouch," Ellery grinned. He did not always win of course—except with this lot. The Monday Night Scrabblers were a lot tougher competition. His old college pals? Not so much. Back in the day, they'd all preferred Clue and Trivial Pursuit.

Flip said, "I don't care that he always wins. I don't want to play because I hate Scrabble."

"Hey, hey, hey. We don't permit that kind of talk in this house." Ellery rose from the sofa. "Who needs another drink?"

Everyone needed a drink. Especially, as Chelsea tactfully put it, *if they were going to have to play games all night.*

"Do you need a hand?" Freddie, like Flip, was not a huge fan of Scrabble. He had been sitting on the sidelines, advising Chelsea.

"Sure," Ellery said.

"I did a quickie interview with your friend at the newspaper," Freddie said as they walked into the kitchen.

"Oh. I don't know if she's actually a friend—or that you need the publicity—but I'm sure you made Sue's day. If not her week."

Freddie smiled in acknowledgement. "I wish I'd had a chance to talk more with Jack. How long did he work in Homicide?"

"I don't know how long he was a detective. He was a cop in L.A. for about ten years."

"I bet he has great stories."

"Probably. He doesn't talk a lot about when he was LAPD." Ellery opened the bottle of light rum. He was making rum runners that evening, which had been one of their summer favorites, back in the day.

"Has he ever killed anyone?"

Ellery stared at Freddie. Freddie's expression was serious.

"Shoot. In the line of duty," Freddie prompted.

"I don't know. I..." Ellery started to answer, *I don't think so*, but realized he really *didn't* know. He suspected that wasn't something Jack would choose to share without good reason. The subject had never come up.

He answered instead, "I hope not. I think that would be really difficult."

"Probably. Although you have to pass a psych test to be a cop. That would be part of what they'd evaluate you for, I guess."

"I guess." Ellery automatically reached for the dark rum. There was *a lot* of booze in a rum runner.

Freddie said very casually, "Are Tosh and Oscar together now?"

Ellery put down the dark rum and measured out the Giffard Creme de Mure with the attention usually reserved for defusing a bomb. He replied carefully, "I think they might have...connected this weekend."

"Yeah." Freddie's laugh was a little bitter. "Turns out Oscar's a fast worker."

Ellery glanced at him in surprise. "Uh, I don't think you could really claim he's a fast worker at this point. We've all know each other for how many years?"

Freddie opened his mouth, but two things happened.

The lights went out, plunging the entire house into darkness—and someone let out a bloodcurdling scream from the library.

Freddie gasped, "Is that Tosh?" and ran for the door.

It sounded like he crashed full force into the kitchen table—and that the entire table went over, table, chairs, and Freddie all hitting the floor.

Arf! Arf! Arf! Whether it was the commotion in the kitchen or the screams in the library, Watson had clearly had enough. He could be heard frantically barking.

Freddie groaned and another chair fell over.

"*Wait*," Ellery called. "Let me get a flashlight!" He felt for the right drawer, found the flashlight, and switched it on. The powerful bright LED beam spotlit Freddie climbing to his feet amidst the toppled chairs and table.

From down the hall everyone in the library seemed to be yelling at the top of their voices. Watson continued to bark hysterically.

He's here...

But even as that terrifying idea formed, Ellery questioned it.

How could he be? How would that be possible?

By the time Ellery and Freddie reached the doorway of the library, the screaming had stopped—that had been Lenny, not Tosh—but Lenny was crying, "I saw a face. I'm telling you. *There was a face in the window*!"

Ellery swung his flashlight over the group standing in the middle of the library. Oscar put his hand up as the beam hit his eyes. Chelsea, still seated on the sofa, looked absolutely petrified. Tosh was hugging Lenny, trying to quiet her. And Flip...

Flip stood near the bookcases at the far end of the room.

"Lenny, there are no windows in this room!" Ellery had to raise his voice to be heard.

But heard he was, because the noise stopped as abruptly as if he'd yanked the plug from a sound system.

Not counting Watson, of course, who continued to bark his outrage at being startled from his deep sleep.

"You were dreaming, Lenny," Tosh said. "You fell asleep on the couch."

"W-w-what?" Lenny faltered. She stared around the walls of bookcases in bewilderment. "I couldn't have!"

"You sure did." Flip's shadow moved to join the others in the circle of light. He grinned at Lenny. "There's not a window in this entire room. There isn't even a mirror."

"*Jeeeeez*," Oscar sat down on the sofa, smoothing his hands over his glossy black hair. "Did my hair just turn white?"

"Are you kidding? Do you even have a single gray hair yet?" Flip asked.

Arf! Arf! Arf!

Chelsea snapped, "Watson, shut up!"

"He's stuck in a loop," Ellery said. "Watson, come here, pal. It's okay." He glanced back at Freddie who still stood behind him. "Are *you* okay?

Freddie's shadow sounded uncharacteristically subdued. "I think I broke your kitchen."

"That's okay. I'm sure that kitchen's survived worse—" Ellery gasped as Watson sprang into his arms, and the flashlight beam swung wildly up, illuminating the painted eyes of the mermaid figurehead above them.

Watson frantically licked Ellery's chin and jaw.

Ellery dodged the tongue. "I know. I know, buddy. Lenny, could this be what you saw?" He pointed the flashlight upwards.

The others gasped. Flip started to laugh. "I was thinking the exact same thing. She sleeps with her eyes half open. Which, by the way, is very creepy, girl."

Lenny stared up, open-mouthed, at the mermaid. Then she shuddered, and let out a shaky giggle. "It was so real in my dream."

Everyone relaxed, laughing nervously, teasing her. Lenny cast another uneasy glance about the room. Shadows from the firelight danced against bookshelves. "I'm sorry, you guys. I never have nightmares."

"It's all the caffeine and rich food," Tosh told her.

Chelsea said, "Yeah, that's it. We've all had too much *caffeine* to drink."

Flip teased, "What kind of witch is afraid of her own dreams?"

Lenny made a face.

The laughter faded as they waited for the lights to come back on.

After a moment or two, Freddie said, "I think that's it for Scrabble."

Tosh went to join Oscar on the sofa. "What time is it?"

"After ten," Ellery answered. "I can get lanterns out if you want to keep playing. The drinks are half made..."

Tactfully, his friends began to demur.

"I don't know," Tosh said vaguely. "I was thinking maybe I'd turn in early tonight. I'm pooped after all that running around in the snow today."

A polite pause followed this while everyone considered Tosh's real plans for the evening.

Oscar gave an evil laugh. "I say, we get flashlights and explore that secret passage—" He winced as Tosh elbowed him.

"What secret passage? Is there a secret passage in this house?" Freddie sounded intrigued.

"No way," Chelsea said hotly. "That's a *horrible* idea. Talk about giving people nightmares! Or someone will break a leg and we won't be able to get help."

No one said anything after that unexpected outburst. Tosh and Oscar somehow managed to look at each other while not looking at each other.

"Okay," Ellery said. "Well, the power might come back on tonight or it might not. We've got plenty of flashlights and candles. If you want to make it an early night, that's fine. If you—"

"We're not leaving tomorrow, are we?" Freddie interrupted.

"I.... It's not looking that way at the moment. If it doesn't snow tonight, and if they can clear the roads tomorrow, and if the ferry starts running—"

"That's a lot of ifs."

"It is."

"Poor Ellery," Flip said. "You didn't realize you were opening a bed and breakfast."

Ellery said honestly, "You know, there are worse things than getting to spend extra time with you guys. I figure we'll just make the best of it."

"Uh oh," Oscar said. "He's going to guilt us into playing Scrabble with him again."

Ellery laughed. "Anyway."

"Anyway, I'm going up," Tosh said briskly, rising.

"I could use an early night," Oscar agreed.

It was hard to tell in the gloom, but Ellery thought Chelsea rolled her eyes.

"Let me get flashlights," Ellery said.

"We've got our phones. No need," Tosh assured him.

Flip said to Lenny, "Shall I see you safely to your boudoir, milady? Those land-locked mermaids are pretty nasty this time of year."

Lenny sniffed. "It's your boudoir, too, bucko."

"Oh, right. You can see me safely up, then."

Freddie's head turned toward Chelsea, who continued to sit in silence on the sofa. He sighed rather heavily. "If you don't mind, I'm going to pour myself a whisky and go up. I've got a script I want to read over."

"Of course," Ellery replied. "I'm going to make myself a nightcap and go up in a bit as well."

"Night, Ell."

"Night." Ellery, still carrying Watson, who seemed uncharacteristically subdued after the evening's excitement, seated himself on the sofa across from Chelsea.

As Freddie's footsteps died away down the hall, Chelsea said, "I thought I'd sit up and enjoy the fire for a while."

"Me, too. Can I fix you a nightcap?"

She shook her head, said shortly, "I wonder how that's going to work out."

"What's that?"

"Tosh and Oscar. Does she think she's fooling anyone?" Chelsea mimicked, "*I'm pooped after all that running around in the snow today!*' Brother."

"Maybe she's just trying to be discreet."

That time there was no mistaking the eye roll.

"They both have fantastic jobs on opposite sides of the country. That is *not* going to last."

Had Chelsea always been so, well, negative? She'd been snarky, yes, but Ellery didn't remember that tinge of mean-spiritedness. But then he and Chelsea hadn't spent a ton of time together on their own. Usually, Ellery had been hanging out with Tosh, and Chelsea had been there, too.

He asked, "What do you do now, Chelsea? Besides act, of course."

Watson gave one of his loud pained moans, and tucked himself into an even tighter ball next to Ellery.

Chelsea said, "Watson said it."

"I mean, we all had to take day jobs," Ellery said.

"Freddie didn't. You didn't."

"My career lasted five minutes. Now I work in a bookstore."

"You made six films. *Movies.* And a slew of commercials. And those stupid movies earned a *ton* of money. And now Black Palace wants you to come back and make *more* of them."

Ellery wasn't quite sure how to respond. The *Happy Halloween! You're Dead* movies had indeed been stupid, but he'd worked hard on them. Even harder after he'd suffered through the first reviews.

Chelsea added, "And you don't just work in a bookstore. You *own* a bookstore. You know what I do? You know what my day job is? Data entry clerk for a hardware company. And I *hate* every minute of it."

"I'm sorry." Which he truly was, because Chelsea was a very good actress. Or had been, back in the day. He was under the impression that she was still getting roles, still getting good reviews, but obviously her career had not taken off as she'd hoped.

Most careers in the arts did not.

"Meanwhile, everything Tosh wants falls in her lap. Even the things she *doesn't* want fall in her lap."

Ellery said nothing. Tosh was talented, hardworking, and personable. Those traits were an advantage in life. He understood that Chelsea needed to vent, and he was sorry for her, but he was acutely uncomfortable sitting there listening to her bash one of their closest friends.

At the same time, he didn't want to leave Chelsea downstairs on her own. For one thing, it didn't seem kind. For another... Well, he hadn't been one hundred percent convinced she'd taken Tosh's pictures. But now he was pretty sure she was trying to outwait him so she could retrieve the box. Once she realized the photos were no longer in the passage, she was going to be very freaked out.

And that, Ellery felt certain, was not going to make the weekend easier for anyone.

"Anyway," Chelsea said, "I don't know why I'm telling you all this. I know you're tired. You don't have to sit up with me."

"No, I'm happy to. We haven't really had a chance to chat this weekend."

"Chatting was never really our thing, was it?"

"No. But I'm happy to lend an ear."

"No worries. You can keep your body parts intact." She intended it for a joke, but he could read the irritation in her eyes.

Chelsea folded her arms and stared at the fire.

Ellery stroked Watson's silky head, said, "Did I miss something? Why the jokes about Lenny and witchcraft?"

Chelsea seemed taken aback. "You don't remember all that occult garbage back at Tisch?"

"I remember she used to tell our fortunes with tarot cards." He smiled faintly. He was pretty sure not a single one of Lenny's predictions had come true.

"It was a lot more than tarot cards. She tried to conjure a demon once."

"Say what?"

"You don't remember when she and Brandon tried to conjure whatever his name was? Leonard, I think."

"Brandon? *My* Brandon? Tried to conjure a demon named *Leonard*?" He was momentarily distracted. "I thought demons were all named stuff like Moloch and Baal?"

Chelsea shrugged. "This one was named Leonard. Or maybe it was Leopold? I forget what his thing was. The great Lord of the Fly, maybe?"

"Lord of the *Fly*," Ellery repeated. "Fly as in insects that buzz around and get on your food? Or fly as in the opening in a pair of jeans?"

"No clue. All I know is they nearly set the dorm on fire."

"I don't remember this at all."

"It might have been one of the weekends you went home. Anyway, I think she outgrew it. Although she still wears that little star pendant."

"Yeah, but lots of people wear pentagrams who aren't trying to summon the Lord of the Flies."

Chelsea shrugged, glanced at the clock on the fireplace. He could feel her rising impatience.

Ellery nodded at the fireplace, half rose and said, "I'm just going to put another log on."

As he'd hoped, that was the last straw.

Chelsea let out an exasperated breath. "Not on my account. I'm going up."

"Oh? Are you?"

"Yes." She rose.

"Okay. Well, good night. Sleep well."

"Night," she said tersely.

He waited until her footsteps had faded, then he asked Watson if he wanted to go outside.

Watson gave him a look of utter disbelief, and settled more comfortably on the sofa.

Ellery chuckled. "Okay. Suits me. Bed time?"

Now he was talking.

Watson sprang from the couch, leading the way down the dark hallway, galloping up the staircase, two steps at a time, and racing into Ellery's bedroom. His moonlit shadow leaped onto the bed, waiting until Ellery pulled the comforter back, and burrowed beneath.

Ellery washed up by the light of his flashlight and joined Watson shortly after.

He'd been hoping Jack might phone, but there were no messages on his cell. Jack was probably spending a cold and wearying night dealing with one small disaster after another. Hopefully, nothing too serious.

He watched a meteor curve across the black bowl of night, followed almost immediately by another bright streak through the sky.

November was a great month for meteor showers. Were these the Taurids or the Leonids? Great-aunt Eudora would surely have known.

Hopefully, the skies would continue to clear—followed by the roads—and Jack would be home tomorrow night.

Watson, a furry footwarmer, was already snoring.

Ellery smiled faintly, his eyelids getting heavier and heavier.

It had been a long day even though it had largely been spent eating, drinking, and having snowball fights, and he was very tired...

He did not remember falling asleep.

But he would not forget waking up to the sound of a woman's screams.

CHAPTER SIXTEEN

Watson began to scramble wildly, his barks muffled beneath the heavy comforter.

Arf. Arf. Arf.

Ellery half fell, half clambered out of the tall bed, and jumped to his feet, managing not to fall over Watson, who had also managed to escape the tangle of bedding. He grabbed his robe, his flashlight, knocked his phone off the nightstand, retrieved his phone and dropped it in his bathrobe pocket, jerked open the door and nearly fell over Watson *again*. Glimmering ghostly figures filled the hallway as doors flew open up and down the long corridor.

"What's going on?"

"Did you hear that?"

"Is that Lenny?"

"Lenny's with me," Flip called from the opposite end of the hall. "That wasn't Lenny."

Arf! Arf! Arf!

Ellery tried flipping on the hall light switch and to his great relief, misty light flooded over them from the frosted glass globe overhead.

Oscar and Tosh, wide-eyed and rumpled, filled the doorway of Oscar's bedroom.

Flip and Lenny stood in the middle of the hall, looking equally bewildered. Lenny clutched the tail end of Flip's New York Athletic Club T-shirt. Flip was clutching a log from the fireplace.

At the top of the stairs, Freddie stood, primed for action but unsure of where to go. He was pale and wore red and blue checkerboard boxers and a navy-blue T-shirt.

Ellery scanned the hall again. *Two, four, five...* "Where's Chelsea?"

Everyone stared at Chelsea's closed door. Even Watson fell silent.

Tosh left Oscar's side and went to Chelsea's room. She thumped on the door.

"Chels? Chelsea?"

No response.

Tosh drew a breath and turned the door handle. "Chelsea? Are you awake?"

"Turn the light on," Freddie ordered. He continued to stare uneasily into the darkness of the hall below.

Ellery moved past Tosh, groping over the wall to find the light switch—before remembering that there was no overhead light in this room. "Hang on."

Heart pounding with instinctive dread, eyes pinned to the dark motionless shape of the bed, he made his way across the room, felt over the nightstand, and turned on the small lamp.

Soft light illuminated the empty sheets.

Chelsea was not in bed. She was not in the room. The bedclothes were rumpled and thrown back. The jeans and sweater she'd worn earlier were draped over the chair by the window. Her phone lay on the nightstand.

"She's not here," he called, which turned out not to be necessary since the others had all nervously crowded into the doorway with Tosh.

"Where is she?" Tosh asked blankly.

Ellery shook his head.

"Where did that scream come from?" Lenny asked.

"Downstairs?" Flip looked at Ellery.

Ellery was not sure. He tried to remember, but of course he had been deeply asleep.

Freddie exclaimed, "Wait a minute. Damn it. This is one of her pranks!"

There were gasps of outrage—and relief.

"Oh, my God!" Tosh sagged against Oscar. "*Yes*." She gave a shaky laugh.

Oscar muttered, "I'll murder her."

Ellery was relieved, too. For about three seconds. Then unease began to creep in again.

Freddie returned to the top of the stairs and called down, "Not funny, Chels!"

No reply.

Would she reply, though?

Flip said, "This is totally like her." And yet, he didn't sound convinced.

Ellery was not convinced either. He joined Freddie at the top of the stairs, and shone his flashlight into the murky darkness at the bottom of the staircase. "Chelsea?"

Still no reply.

"I'll go down and look for her." He was not thrilled at the idea.

To his relief, Freddie said, "I'll go with you."

"We'll all go," Flip chimed in. "We can cover more ground that way."

"Serve her right if we all went back to bed," Oscar said under his breath.

There was a murmur of agreement, but Tosh said, "No. She might have slipped and fallen or tripped over something in the dark..."

Ellery started cautiously down the staircase, Watson right on his heels, Freddie and the others a few steps behind.

"Be careful on the stairs," Ellery warned. "Watson leaves his toys here sometimes."

Midway down the staircase, his flashlight illuminated empty gleaming floor and the closed and secured front door.

Nothing appeared to be amiss.

He reached the bottom and turned on the wall switch.

The softly prismed light of the chandelier revealed the somber faces in the old portraits—and the worried faces of his friends.

Everything seemed reassuringly normal.

Nothing—and no one—was out of place. Well, not counting Chelsea.

There was a collective sigh of relief from Freddie, Oscar, Tosh, Flip, and Lenny.

"If she's *not* pulling some stupid practical joke," Flip said, "What would she be doing down here?"

Ellery and Tosh exchanged startled looks of realization.

"I'm going to check the library," Ellery said. "If you guys want to take a look at the other rooms..."

"I'll go with you," Tosh said.

"Me, too," said Oscar.

In the end, they all accompanied Ellery down the hall to the library.

The room was dark; the double doors stood wide open.

Ellery strode inside, turned on the lights. The wooden mermaid gazed down upon the empty room. Throw blankets and accent pillows were in disarray. Laptops sat open on the low chests, empty and half-filled glasses beside them. The Scrabble board lay on the center chest. In short, everything was exactly as they'd left it.

There was no sign of Chelsea.

No sign anyone had entered the room after Ellery had gone up to bed.

And yet...

With each passing moment, Ellery's disquiet ratcheted up, notch by notch.

"She's not here," Flip said.

They began to back out again. Ellery stared at the book-cases at the far end of the room. His scalp prickled.

Oh, no. Oh, God.

At the same instant, Tosh, directly behind him, gasped a soft, "Oh, *no*."

Once again, the door to the secret passage was ajar.

Watson, huff raised and crouching low to the ground, cautiously approached the opening. That alone was enough to warn Ellery.

He called sharply, "*Watson, no.*"

Watson scurried back, tail between his legs.

Slowly, dread mounting with each unwilling footstep, Ellery walked to the bookcase. He used his elbow to nudge the door wide.

A weird and alarming odor reached his nostrils—the usual moldering damp combined with something new, something he was unfortunately beginning to recognize.

He braced himself, his gaze following the bright beam of light to—

"No. *No...* Oh, *hell.*" Ellery stepped hastily back, leaning against the bookshelf, closing his eyes against that terrible sight.

Tosh half-screamed, "She *can't* be!"

Ellery's eyes snapped open. "Everybody out," he said thickly.

His friends stared at him, stupid and stricken with horror.

"*Out.* Now. Don't touch anything. Don't move anything."

Pulling himself together, Ellery moved toward them, gesturing toward the doors.

"Come on, gang," Freddie began to back up. "It looks like this is a crime scene."

Lenny cried, "*Edwin Dolph is in the house*!"

Ellery went rigid. Lenny was right. Why hadn't that occurred to him?

But even as the thought occurred, he was questioning it. Even if Dolph had made it to land, he'd almost certainly have died of exposure. Besides, Watson knew when a squirrel was inside the walls. How could he possibly not know a stranger was hiding in the house?

"We don't know that."

"Of *course,* it was Dolph," Tosh protested. "What are you saying?"

What *was* he saying? And how dumb was he that he was saying it aloud?

"No, you're right," he said quickly. As frightening as that thought was, he really wanted to believe Chelsea had been killed by Edwin Dolph—versus the alternative.

But would Dolph, knowing there was a whole house full of people to contend with, leave the hatchet behind?

The image of what he'd just glimpsed in the passageway flashed into his mind. A wave of nausea rose in Ellery's throat. He was saved, not by masculine pride, but by the recollection of how expensive it had been to get these antique rugs cleaned.

"Out," he repeated weakly, and everyone filed into the hallway.

"What are we going to do?" Lenny looked terrified. Granted, they all looked varying degrees of shocked and scared. It was the normal reaction.

"You're going to stay together right here. Nobody goes anywhere. I'm going to call Jack and get directions on what to do about..."

Everything, frankly.

Tosh, Oscar, Flip, Lenny, and Freddie stared at him blankly.

And then there were five...

Well, actually six.

Seven, counting Watson.

And possibly, though he was doubting it more and more with each passing minute, eight.

It seemed unlikely.

As much as he did not want to believe it, it felt more and more likely that one of *them*...

"Wait right here. Watson, *stay*," Ellery ordered, and stepped back inside the library closing the doors firmly behind him.

Watson immediately began to scratch at the doors, ignoring the chorus of, "Come on, puppy! Come on, sweet doggie!"

Ellery moved away from the doors. Warily watching the entrance to the passage, he pulled his phone out, pressing Jack's number as he walked slowly toward the opening.

"Carson," Jack snapped on the first ring. Up and about at three in the morning? No wonder he was curt. Jack's tone changed. "*Oh.* Sorry. What's going on?"

"Something..." Ellery's voice shook. Something to do with the relief of managing to reach Jack so quickly? Or was it just the sound of Jack's voice? He got control fast. "...really awful happened. Chelsea's dead."

"*Dead?* Are you okay? Is anyone else—"

"We're all fine. Jack, she was hit in the head with the hatchet."

Jack swore very quietly. "When?"

"It must have just happened. We all heard her scream and ran downstairs. I found her in the passage that leads from the library. We think Edwin Dolph is in the house."

"No." Jack sounded absolutely certain.

"*No?*"

"No. Dolph's body was found late yesterday evening. The current carried it down to the rocks below the light-house at Half Moon Bay."

Ellery could think of nothing to say. Half Moon Bay was all the way on the other side of the island.

Into his silence, Jack added, "It might be better not to share that information."

"But everyone's scared out of their wits. I can't let them go on thinking—"

Jack said austerely, "Not everyone."

Ellery swallowed. Right. Because if Dolph hadn't murdered Chelsea, someone—one of Ellery's oldest friends—had.

Which was absolutely unthinkable.

Jack interrupted these painful reflections. "Ellery, I'm sorry to do this to you, but I need to see the—Chelsea's body."

Ellery closed his eyes. Opened them. "Okay."

"I'm not going to be able to get anybody out there for a few hours. The road to Captain's Seat is still not passable."

"Yes. I know."

"I'm s— Also, you're going to have to secure the crime scene."

"Right."

"But first—"

"Yes." Ellery continued to the door to the interior passageway.

"I'm going to need photos from as many angles as you can get." Jack sounded insanely normal, even prosaic. "But be careful where you step and don't touch anything, don't move anything." He added, "Don't *remove* anything, either."

Ellery understood why Jack might think he needed that extra cautioning, and he did not take offense.

"Mm-hm."

Feeling more than a little queasy, he took as many photos as he could, until Jack said he thought he had enough.

"Good. You're doing great."

Ellery had no response.

"You're not going to like this," Jack said. "But I want you to very lightly touch her inner wrist to check for temperature. Do not move her, do not disturb the scene any more than you have to."

"Yes." Ellery gritted his teeth, knelt, and delicately touched Chelsea's upturned wrist. "Sorry," he murmured, and then jerked his hand back in shock. "She's *cool.*"

"How cool?" Jack sounded startled.

"N-N-noticeably cool. But it *just* happened."

"Cold or cool?"

"Cool." Ellery stared down the dark passage. "I mean, it's cold and damp in here, but even so. We *just* heard her scream."

"Noted. It's now 3:47. Okay. Anything else out of the ordinary?"

"Like what? There's a hatchet in her head!"

"Okay," Jack said soothingly. "Listen, I know this is hard. But your help is crucial."

"It can't have been more than forty-five minutes since she screamed."

"I've made a note. Now I want you to remove yourself from the scene. I want you to close the passage. I want you to leave everything in the library exactly as it is, and I want you to lock the library doors and block them with furniture. No one is to enter that room until I can get a crime scene team from the mainland out there."

"Yes. Okay."

"Then I want you to block off the other entrance to that passageway and lock the cellar door."

"Got it. But if Dolph is dead, no one is going to come out of those tunnels."

"You and I know that. No one else needs to."

"Yes. Right." They'd covered this already. His brain seemed to be moving in slow motion.

"Next, you're going to need to confiscate everyone's electronics."

"Uhhhh..."

"I know, but we don't want any data erased and we don't want them communicating with each other after you tell them to isolate in their rooms.

"After I—That is *not* going to go over well."

"Explain to them that it's necessary to prevent any communication that could interfere with the investigation."

"I can explain that to them until I'm blue in the face, but I don't think they're going to care. I don't think they'll want to cooperate when they think there's a crazed killer running loose, and I can't exactly blame them."

"I know, but we need to prevent them from talking and potentially contaminating each other's testimony."

Ellery didn't continue to argue, but Jack really did not get the current mood at Captain's Seat.

"Obviously, Chelsea's room is off limits—you'll have to lock it up as well—but we want everyone in a separate room, if possible. I know there aren't enough bedrooms—"

"Wait a minute," Ellery objected. "How am I supposed to convince them that even though Edwin Dolph is still on the loose, they all need to isolate? Because that's the *last* thing we'd be doing, if Dolph was actually a threat. There's safety in numbers and we all know it."

Jack was silent for a moment.

He sighed. "Okay. You're right. It's going to be difficult in these circumstances to keep them separated. You'll have to get them to agree not to discuss what's happened amongst themselves."

Ellery assented doubtfully.

"I'll have to have you collect initial statements from everyone." Jack sounded like he was thinking aloud. "Yeah, that'll work. Record the interviews on your phone. Get them to tell you where they were and what they were doing from the point each of them went to bed."

Ellery bit back a slightly hysterical laugh. "That should make for enlivening listening."

"Make it clear that a more thorough questioning will follow once the CSI team arrives, and that they are *not* to discuss anything related to Chelsea's death."

"I'll try, Jack. I just don't know how practical it is to ask that. Everyone is shocked and upset and scared. They're going to talk. They *need* to talk."

Jack sighed. "I know. Believe me. But at the very least, warn them they *cannot* talk to each other about this until you've taken those initial statements. That's not too much self-control to ask for."

It wasn't, no. But it was liable to be more than his friends were capable of at the moment. Ellery didn't say that, though. He could feel Jack's frustration and worry. And that frustration and worry was understandable.

Jack's tone changed. "Ellery, you need to be very careful. If there was any other way to get what I need done, I wouldn't be putting you front and center on someone's radar. But there isn't. So please do everything you can to make it seem like you're just following orders. Collect the information and let them know that it's going straight to me. Do not, under any circumstances, pursue any angle or line of inquiry on your own. Please promise me that."

For once that was an easy promise to make.

"I give you my word. The last thing I want to do is find out one of my friends is capable of-of murder."

Jack returned tersely, "Yeah, well one of your friends is *more* than capable. So don't forget it."

CHAPTER SEVENTEEN

The request to hand over electronics went about as well as Ellery had imagined it would.

And, as he'd anticipated, explaining Jack's reasoning made zero difference.

"How are we going to influence or contaminate each other's recollections when we don't *know* anything?" Tosh questioned. "We were all in bed."

There was no way to argue with that without revealing that Edwin Dolph was dead and someone—a member of their close-knit circle—had murdered Chelsea.

Conscious of Jack's warning to stay off the killer's radar, Ellery had no choice but to pretend to be in agreement.

"I think Jack's just following standard procedure," he explained. It sounded lame to his own ears.

"I'm sure that's true," Freddie agreed. "This is exactly what we did in an episode of *LAPD Blues*. Detective Bolton and his team are in Alaska and they get caught up in a local murder investigation. The small-town cops insist they all stay in their own motel rooms, and of course the killer tries to pick them off one by one."

"Great," Flip muttered. "Can't wait for that part."

Tosh said, "But it's not standard procedure for *us*. We're not murder suspects."

"Why would we make it easier for someone to pick us off one by one?" Lenny asked, which was a reasonable question.

Seeing that he was not going to win this battle, Ellery had to let it go.

However, when it came to blocking off the secret passage entrances in the cellar and the hidden room off the dining room, that was a different matter. He got full and enthusiastic cooperation in stacking boxes and barrels in the cellar, and tables, chairs and chests in the dining room.

"If he's still in there, he's not getting out," Oscar said with bleak satisfaction as the last dining room chair was stacked onto the precarious tower of furniture cutting off access to the hidden closet.

Flip said, "The problem is, even Ellery doesn't know how many passages there are in this house. Or where they all lead."

"Thanks for sharing that thought out loud," Lenny said.

Flip shrugged. "It's the truth. If we're going to survive, we have to be realistic."

Ellery said hastily, "I'm *sure* we're going to survive. What sense would it make for Dolph to come after us? He's probably long gone by now."

"What sense did it make for him to go after Chelsea? The guy is crazy, Ell. I don't think he's worried about making good choices."

"I don't understand what Chelsea was doing down here," Lenny said thoughtfully. "And she had to be down here because if he'd dragged her out of her room, that would have created a *huge* ruckus."

"Right. True," Ellery said weakly. He hated lying even when he had good material. This material? Spun of cobwebs and Jack's hopeful delusions.

"So why did she come down to the library?"

"Maybe she couldn't sleep?" Flip suggested. "Maybe she was looking for something to read."

Of course, this was exactly what Jack didn't want: his cast of suspects putting their heads together to work out plausible explanations for everything that had happened.

By then it was almost five a.m., though you'd never know it by looking out the window. The only light, as far as the eye could see, came from moonlight glimmering on snow.

"Why don't I take everyone's initial statements, send them off to Jack, and you can all go back to bed for a while," Ellery suggested. He tried to interpret the expressions on the faces turned his way, and qualified, "Or not."

"*Seriously*?" Lenny asked. "You think we're going to be able to sleep after this?"

"Well, let me get your statements and we can fix breakfast?"

"Who *are* you?" Tosh demanded. "What have you done to our kind-hearted friend Ellery? Are you saying you could *eat* something?"

"I'm not hungry," Ellery admitted, "but it could be a while before help arrives. We probably should keep our strength up."

"Ellery's right," Oscar added, "Also, I'm a stress eater. So yes, I'm hungry."

Tosh sighed. "I don't know about food, but I admit I could use a drink about now."

Ellery said quickly, "Okay. Let's get this statement thing over with. It shouldn't take long. And then I'll make Irish coffees and we can figure out what to do next."

Freddie said, "I think it's important that we all stick together as much as possible. No one should be alone."

This idea was greeted with approval all around. Ellery and Tosh went into the kitchen and the others headed for the front room to wait their turn to be interrogated—and no doubt discuss in detail everything that had happened so far.

The kitchen was still a mess from the night before. The overturned table and chairs lay on the floor. The counter was cluttered with dirty glasses, bottles of alcohol, and an ice bucket full of water.

Ellery fed Watson, who, unlike some of the other members of their party, was definitely in the mood for breakfast. Then he and Tosh righted the table and sat down. He turned his phone on record.

"Sunday, November 16. Interview with Tosh—er, Theresa Chase-Ames. Okay, it was about 10:15 when you and Oscar went upstairs last night. What did you do?"

Tosh began to splutter. "You really want me to share *that* with the at-home audience?"

Ellery sighed. "No, I mean, did you go straight to Oscar's room or did you—"

"We went straight to Oscar's room. I didn't feel like washing up in the dark. Honestly, I was kind of creeped out by everything that happened yesterday. Chelsea stealing my photos, the power going off the way it did. I just wanted to cuddle up some place warm and quiet, and not have to be polite to Chelsea—which I feel horrible saying aloud." Tosh closed her eyes tight and then blinked rapidly. "Anyway, we went to Oscar's room and opened the drapes and the moonlight was really bright and the snow was very pretty. It was cozy, nice, and we talked for a long time and then, you know, and then we went to sleep."

Ellery opened his mouth and Tosh said, "I never woke up until Chelsea screamed. But I think I would have if Oscar had left the bed. The floorboard on his side of the bed squeaks. In fact, the whole bed squeaks when you move around." She cleared her throat. "As one does."

"Right. So, you didn't hear anything weird—"

"We heard everyone else coming up to bed, sure, but I didn't hear anything *weird* until that scream." Tosh studied him curiously. "I know, if this was an ordinary investigation, I'd be under suspicion because of the-the bickering with Chelsea. But you know that's all it was. We were on each other's nerves. There's no mystery. We know who killed her. And even if we didn't, I wouldn't have killed her for taking my photos. Even if I *hadn't* got them back safely."

"I know." Ellery was pretty sure Jack didn't want his opinion on the interview recordings, but he *did* know what Tosh meant. "Do you think anyone else would have wanted to get rid of Chelsea?"

Tosh seemed flabbergasted. "Get *rid* of her? No. Of course not. Get *away* from her, sure. I think she put everyone's back up, one way or the other, this weekend. But we *know* who did it."

Ellery remembered Jack's warning, and said, "True. Okay. I think that's everything. Is there anything you want to add or that you think I should I know?"

Tosh shook her head. Was she suddenly avoiding his gaze?

"Do you want to send Oscar in?"

Tosh nodded, left the room, and Oscar took her place at the table a couple of minutes later.

"Maybe you should have Freddie do this," he joked. "He's out there explaining police procedure to us as according to the scriptwriters of *LAPD Blues.*

Ellery snorted, turned his phone recorder back on. "Sunday, November 16. Interview with Oscar Murillo."

Oscar spread his hands like, *bring it.*

"Okay, so Jack is just interested in what happened when we all went our separate ways last night. You and Tosh went upstairs together. Were either of you on your own at any time after that?"

"I used the john at one point. That took, like, a couple of minutes. We weren't apart at any other time for the rest of the night."

"Were you sleeping?"

"Yes."

"How do you know you weren't apart, if you were asleep?" Ellery pointed out.

"Okay. She was sleeping. I was mostly awake." Oscar made a face. "The truth is, I spent most of the night staring out the window, wondering how we're going to handle this. I'm in L.A. She's in New York. How do we make it work?"

Ellery's brows shot up. "I didn't realize this was—" Serious. He'd sort of assumed that Tosh and Oscar were just enjoying a little, er, auld lang syne.

"I always thought Tosh was terrific," Oscar said. "But she was with Freddie and I was with Belle. The timing was never right. And then we were on opposite sides of the country. Which we still are."

"Right. Well... So, neither of you left the room at any time during the night?"

"Correct."

"Do you know if anyone else left their room?"

"Chelsea was in and out of her room."

Ellery cocked his head. "Was she? When?"

"Right after she came upstairs, I heard her go next door to Freddie's room. I heard them talking and laughing. I heard her go back to her room. Then I heard Freddie on the phone. To his agent, I think. That's how it sounded to me."

"I didn't think the walls were that thin."

"Freddie's used to projecting to the back row, I guess. Anyway, it was still early on the West Coast. They talked for a long time. I kind of lost track because Tosh and I were...more focused on each other at that point."

"Gotcha."

"I did hear Chelsea leave her room again, but I don't know what time it was. She didn't go to back to Freddie— although she did the night before."

"*Did* she?"

"Yeah. I think she stayed, but I couldn't swear to it."

"Right. But last night, she didn't go back to Freddie's room?"

"No. I heard her trying to tiptoe down the hall, but there's no missing those squeaky floorboards. Best guess? She was on her way downstairs."

"You don't know what time that was?"

"No. It was still relatively early, though. She was going after Tosh's photos, I bet."

Probably. That would be Ellery's bet, too.

"Did you hear her come back?"

"No."

"Did you hear anyone else leave their room?"

"No. Well, I think I finally dozed off about then. Because it was a lot later and I was sound asleep when I heard that scream. It scared the hell out of me. I thought it was Tosh for a second."

Ellery felt a flicker of alarm. "But Tosh hadn't left the room, right?"

"No. She was sound asleep until then." Oscar smiled faintly. "She has the cutest little snore. But no. The scream scared her awake, too."

Freddie was up next.

"I know exactly how this works," he assured Ellery, as he took his seat at the table. "I've been getting a lot of coaching from Dan Moran."

"*Ah*," said Ellery who'd never heard of Dan Moran in his life.

"Dan's a lieutenant with LAPD. He's not on the Murder Squad, but he's a detective. He's married to Sean Fairchild."

"Oh. The guy who won last year for *The Charioteer*?"

"The guy who won everything last year. Right. Anyway, he's a police procedural consultant for the studio. Dan, I mean. So, I know what you should ask."

"Great," Ellery said. "Because I feel really awkward doing this."

Watson, head on Ellery's foot, let out one of those groans at what he clearly considered one of Ellery's least convincing performances.

"Nah. It's fine." Freddie nodded to Ellery's phone. "You want to get going?"

"Yep." Ellery turned on the recorder. "Sunday, November 16. Interview with Freddie Ames."

"You should probably add the time," Freddie advised.

"Right. 5:45 a.m. Okay. Well, the obvious question is, did you hear or see anything weird or suspicious last night?"

"No." Freddie amended, "Until Chelsea screamed this morning."

"How'd you sleep?"

"Really well. It's so quiet out here. And that's a great mattress."

"After you went upstairs—"

"I was reading a script for a movie my agent wants me to audition for. But reading by flashlight is pretty hard on the eyes, and then Chelsea came by."

"What time was that?"

"I didn't check the time," Freddie said apologetically. "I don't think I'd been reading for even an hour."

"Was she just saying goodnight or...?"

Freddie gave a short laugh. "You're so diplomatic. No. We'd hooked up the night before, and I think she wanted to give it another go-round. But I was beat. Then she reminded me that I was going to talk to my agent about taking her on as a client when she gets to L.A."

"Was she upset that you didn't want to spend the night together?"

Freddie chuckled. "No. It wasn't like that between us. Honestly, I think that was just an excuse to remind me to phone my agent. Chelsea's really ambitious. Which I respect because so am I. Plus, she's—she was—really talented. I feel like it's important to pay it forward."

Ellery met Freddie's steadfast blue gaze. It had never occurred to him before how much he resembled Freddie on *Scooby-Doo*. Now he couldn't unsee it.

"It is. She was," he agreed vaguely. He couldn't help thinking that Freddie's acting had improved considerably, because whatever Freddie thought—or pretended to think— no way had Chelsea's feelings for him been anywhere near as casual as his feelings for her.

Freddie said regretfully, "That was the last time I saw her. I still can't get over it."

"It's pretty shocking. Did you happen to notice the time when she left your room?"

"If the lights had been on, I'd probably have noticed. But the lights were off and I didn't think to check because...why would I? I didn't know I'd need an alibi."

Ellery said quickly, "It's not that anybody needs an alibi. We know who...who killed her. But." Inspiration struck.

"Dolph will presumably deny everything. Even if he doesn't, a lawyer will try to build a defense for him. Which means it's just like you said. Standard procedure."

"What I'll never understand is why she'd go down there," Freddie said. "Especially when it was pitch dark. No offense, but this place is pretty spooky at night. The way the wind moans down the fireplace, and the little drafts from unexpected places, and all the squeaking beams and creaking plumbing. Give me mid-century modern any day."

"It grows on you."

"I'll take your word for it."

"Did you hear her go downstairs?"

"No. I must have been asleep by then."

"Did you leave your room at any time?"

Freddie shook his head. "After I talked to Sid—my agent—I went to bed. It's not like you can do a lot in the dark." He added a little bitterly, "Not without company."

If Oscar could hear everything going on in Freddie's room, the reverse had to be true.

"Mm." Ellery looked apologetic.

Freddie scowled. "I mean, it's not like— It was over between me and Tosh a long time ago. But I still love her, of course. She's a great girl. I want her to be happy. And Oscar's a nice guy. But no way is *that* going to last. Not in a million years."

"Yeah," Ellery said absently. "You can never predict what attracts people to each other."

Freddie laughed. "That's the truth! You're the last person I imagined would end up with a cop. Let alone the chief of police."

"I think Jack's the most shocked of anybody," Ellery deadpanned, and that was strictly for Jack's benefit.

"Anyway, listening to the carnival next door didn't put me in the greatest mood, so I just went to sleep."

"Before you fell asleep, did you hear anybody else leave their room?"

Freddie slowly shook his head, but said, "Maybe Oscar? I heard someone walk down the hallway. It could have been Chelsea. Or it could have been Oscar. I think it was right next door. I'm not sure."

Ellery studied him. "Right next door? Then it could have been Tosh?"

Freddie stared at him. "No. Not Tosh. It was probably Chels."

Probably.

Freddie added, "Seeing that Chelsea ended up downstairs."

"True."

Freddie grimaced. "Anyway. That was it for me. I don't remember another thing until I heard that scream this morning." He shuddered. "I couldn't remember where I was for a second."

"I know the feeling." Ellery said slowly, "Well, you're the expert. Can you think of anything else I should ask or that Jack should know?"

Freddie's expression brightened. "Beyond accounting for our movements, no. We know who our perp is. Now it's just a matter of finding him—before he strikes again."

CHAPTER EIGHTEEN

"That *before he strikes again* comment, worries me," Ellery admitted, wishing he'd worn ear muffs. The wind was bitterly cold.

He was on his cell phone, standing in the garden—which currently resembled the courtyard of an ice palace—watching Watson fall into snow drift after snow drift.

"Yeah, I don't care much for that." Jack sounded bleak—and very far away. "Are you thinking we should be looking closely at Freddie?"

"I haven't even talked to Flip or Lenny yet. But... He did seem pretty disingenuous through a lot of that interview. He was definitely considering throwing Oscar under the bus, until he realized it meant throwing Tosh, too. I think he still loves her."

"Maybe. As much as a narcissist is capable of."

A lump of snow fell from a tree and splattered Watson's head. Watson looked indignantly around for the culprit.

Ellery said, "You think Freddie's a narcissist?"

"In fairness, I met Ames once. I'm not in a position to psychoanalyze him. I'm more interested in your thoughts."

"I think anyone who plans on a career in the arts has to be a *little* bit of an egotist."

"I guess that explains why you prefer selling books."

"For a lot of reasons."

Watson, having decided the headless Cupid near the frozen ornamental pond had lobbed a snowball at him, began to shout accusations.

"Language," Ellery admonished. Watson wagged his tail and returned to slandering Cupid for all to hear.

Ellery said, "Any news on when some actual detectives might be out this way?"

"Murder trumps just about everything else, so the snowplows are headed to you now. But we're talking about clearing a lot of heavy, wet snow and ice on narrow country lanes, so it will be a couple of hours at least."

"What about a forensics team from the mainland?"

"No ferry. No helicopters. There's supposed to be another storm moving in."

"No."

Jack said quickly, "Someone will get to you today. I promise. If I have to hike out there myself."

Poor Jack. This was probably even harder on him. Ellery sealed his lips on everything he wanted to say, none of which would be particularly useful.

"It's okay. I know you're doing everything you can. I'll get back in there and finish up with Lenny and Flip. And then..."

And then he had no idea.

"I'm sorry, you're having to deal with this on your own." Jack sounded troubled. "I should be there."

"And you should be right where you are, too. You can't be everywhere, Jack. I'm not *enjoying* this, but it's under control."

So far.

Jack made a sound of exasperation, and said, "I'll listen to these interviews. Send me the recordings of Flip and Lenny as soon as you've got them."

Ellery said, "I will. Did you happen to hear back from NYPD yet?"

"Not yet. Does that mean you think Chelsea's murder might be connected to Noah's death?"

Ellery said wearily, "It must be, right? Chelsea's death has to somehow tie in with Tosh's photos, because I can't think of any other reason for her to sneak downstairs in the middle of the night. Which forces me to believe that Tosh's photos must reveal something to do with Noah's death."

"I agree."

"But we all went through those photos. Even you looked through those photos. I didn't see anything incriminating or revealing. Did you? I saw a bunch of pics of dumbass kids having a lot of fun pretending to be adults."

Jack said sternly. "You were adults. Young adults, but old enough to know right from wrong."

"But there was nothing in the photos, Jack. What could there have been, anyway? There were only a handful of photos of Noah."

"I don't know," Jack admitted. "You're right. I didn't see anything incriminating or revealing. But something has to be there."

"Well, when I'm done with Flip and Lenny, I'll take another look."

"*No*," Jack said quickly. "Leave that for the professionals. When the interviews are finished, so are you. As far as any further investigating goes, I mean."

"Thanks for clarifying."

"The last thing you want to do—or that I want you to do—is give the impression that you're questioning anything that's happened so far."

Ellery said with exasperation, "Then I'll be the only one."

There was a short silence and the muffled sound of someone talking in the background. Jack came back on. "I've got to go. Please be careful. I can't stress that enough."

"I will be. I love you."

"I love you, too. Very much. So please don't take any chances. I'll be there as soon as I can."

Ellery opened his mouth—

Dial tone.

Ellery sighed, clicked off, and whistled to Watson.

"**L**enny and I've been talking," Flip said, when he sat down for his interview. "We're *convinced* Chelsea's murder has to do with Noah's accident."

Jack's warnings still ringing in his ears, Ellery could only manage a feeble, "Uhhhh... Did you discuss that theory in front of everyone?"

"Give us *some* credit," Flip scoffed. "Of course not. Like everybody else, we're pretending that we think Edwin Dolph is scurrying around inside the walls like a demented squirrel."

"Lenny didn't seem to be pretending this morning."

"She was half-awake. We all were. But now that we've had time to think it through, come on. Why would Dolph come here in the first place? You made that case pretty effectively when we were initially worried about his showing up. Secondly, if he *did* come here, why would he skulk around in the secret passages waiting for someone to show up so he could kill them? Why wouldn't he come out during the night and murder us all in our beds like a normal axe murderer?"

"You put that so well," Ellery said.

"I'm serious. Why wasn't he stealing food from the kitchen? Why hasn't Watson been barking his head off? He's not here and you know it."

"I don't know it for a fact. And neither do you."

Flip opened his mouth, and Ellery said very quietly, "Think, Flip. If you *are* right about a connection between Chelsea and Noah, is it smart to make a point of there being no alternative culprit besides one of us?"

Flip blinked. "*Oh.*"

"Exactly."

Flip leaned forward and whispered, "I remembered something that happened a couple of days before Noah died."

Ellery moved his phone closer to Flip. "What?"

Flip looked over his shoulder and whispered, "Not here. Not now. I don't want to say—"

Ellery's jaw dropped. "*Flip*! You've got to be kidding me. Are you out of your *mind*?"

Flip gave a shaky laugh. "Totally joking. Of *course,* I'm going to say. It's just that it feels like one of those old movies where somebody knows a vital piece of evidence, but d—"

Ellery burst out, "*You're joking around in the middle of a murder*?"

Flip looked sheepish. "Sorry! I'm just nervous. This whole situation feels like we're in a Fellini film."

Or a Woody Allen movie.

Ellery said forbiddingly, "Phillip Daly, do you have information or not?"

"Yes! I was remembering that before... before Noah died, he was...not edgy, but maybe a little stressed. When I asked him what was wrong, he said he was going to have a conversation he didn't want to have."

"With whom?"

"He wouldn't say."

"Did he say what the conversation was about?"

"No. He only said it was awkward."

"Awkward?" Ellery repeated.

"Wait. No. He said it was *difficult*. It was going to be difficult. That's it. I think."

"You're not sure?"

"I'm not sure of the exact word he used. Maybe it *was* awkward. But I *am* sure that it was just a day or two before he died. *That*, I'm positive about."

At the time, Ellery had been living with Noah and Flip. Brandon had been there off and on, and Brandon was always a distraction, but not so much of a distraction that Ellery wouldn't have noticed if Noah was especially stressed.

At least, he didn't think so. Or would he?

It was hard to say.

"You don't have *any* idea what the conversation was about? Or who he was going to talk to?"

Flip's expression was regretful. He shook his head. "I don't think Noah wanted me to know until he'd spoken to the person. That's the impression I got."

"I don't remember anything about this."

"Neither does Lenny." Flip sighed.

"You didn't tell the police about it after Noah was killed?"

"Tell them what? That Noah mentioned he was going to have an awkward conversation with someone? It wasn't like he was afraid or that he thought there would be trouble. He was uncomfortable and he thought it would be awkward. Or difficult."

Ellery cast his thoughts back to that time and that place, but none of this rang a bell.

"Do you remember anything going on back then that might have been the reason for Noah's talk with this unknown person?"

"No. But I know that person had to be one of us. Or why not tell me the name? It had to be because it was someone I knew."

Ellery glanced at the little numbers clicking past on his phone. Jack was *not* going to be happy with direction of this interview. But wasn't this the very kind of thing that Jack *needed* to know?

"How serious could this conversation have been if none of us can remember anything that was going on at the time?"

Flip shrugged. "I know. I agree. But it popped into my mind last night and now I can't think of anything else."

What the heck could that awkward conversation have been in regard to? What were the usual conflicts they'd had? Borrowing something without asking, eating the last of something, skipping out on household chores, not paying their fair share of a utility bill? Kid stuff.

The other problem with that theory was Ellery and Flip and, yes, sometimes Brandon, had been Noah's roommates, and none of them had any problem speaking up if they thought somebody wasn't pulling their weight. It wouldn't require special *awkward* conversations.

What then?

Had Noah become aware of something outside their own small household? But within their tight circle of friends?

But what?

"Okay. Well, it's all here for Jack to consider. As far as your movements last night?"

"I made no movements. I was dead to the world the minute my head hit the pillow. The last thing I remember was Lenny speculating on whether Chelsea was going to have another try for Freddie." Flip added a little wearily, "Poor Chelsea."

"You didn't hear anyone moving around last night?"

"No."

"And you wouldn't know if Lenny left your room."

Flip gave a short laugh. "No. Way. Lenny's a little scaredy cat. No way would my girl wander around this place at night. And, by the way, Lenny's half the size of Chelsea. How the heck would she have overpowered her?"

Ellery met Flip's gaze. "You don't need a lot of strength to use a hatchet."

Flip swallowed. "*Oh*. She was hit from behind. God." He looked sick.

Ellery also felt sick when he remembered the image of Chelsea lying there in the passageway. But no, she had not been hit from behind. She'd been facing her attacker when she'd been struck. She had seen it coming—though not in time.

Which Flip did not know.

Which meant here was someone he could scratch off his list of suspects?

Ellery clicked off the recorder. "Okay, you want to send Lenny in?"

"**D**id Flip tell you what we think?" Lenny asked, as soon as Ellery finished stating her name and the date for the recording.

Ellery groaned inwardly. "Please, *please* tell me you two aren't discussing this where anyone can hear you?"

Lenny gave him a chiding look.

Ellery was not reassured. "Let's say you and Flip are right. You both *have* to know how dangerous it is to even hint that you think Chelsea's death might be tied to...something that happened back when we were in college."

"We're not hinting. We're speaking to you in private. But it makes sense, right?"

Ellery sighed. "It's a good theory, yes, but we don't have any proof of anything. We don't even know for sure that Noah's death wasn't an accident. Let alone that Chelsea's death is somehow tied to Noah's."

"But the odds of it being a coincidence have to be astronomical. Don't you think?"

"Do *I* think so?" Ellery grimaced. "Yes. I don't *want* to think it, but... I can't come up with any reason one of us would want Chelsea dead. She wasn't...her best self this weekend, but she wasn't doing anything that would drive someone to commit murder."

Lenny said meaningfully, "That we know of."

"Right."

"Which means we have to figure out what Chelsea did last night that made someone decide they had to kill her."

"Lenny, for the love of God."

She brushed that aside. "What does Jack say?"

"It'll still be a few hours before anyone can reach us."

"No, about our *case*."

Ellery was pretty sure his hair stood on end as he experienced a frightening moment of déjà vu. It was like being confronted with a baby version of Nora.

"*We* don't have a case!" he hissed. "We're just collecting information so that Jack can build *his* case. Which would have to be something that could hold up in court."

"*Exactly.*" She hissed back. "We're helping him do that. You do this all the time, right?"

"Not *this*! This is a completely different situation. For one thing, I'm not usually playing eenie meenie miny mo with the lives of my oldest friends."

"But—"

"Lenny, stop. It's not a game. You and Flip don't seem to understand—"

She said indignantly, "I know it's not a game! *We* know it's not a game. Don't you see? Our best chance of making sure we don't all end up like poor Chelsea is to figure out why he killed her."

Ellery stared. "He?"

Lenny's face scrunched up in pain. "*Ell*, you're not going to pretend you don't know who killed Chelsea? There's only one real possibility, and you know it. We *all* know it. We might not want to believe it, but who else could it be?"

CHAPTER NINETEEN

Ellery was ransacking the contents of the counter drawer designated "Watson's stuff" when Tosh walked into the kitchen.

"I thought I'd lend a hand with the Irish—" She stopped in her tracks, frowning. "What are you doing?"

Ellery, clutching a small plastic pill bottle, jumped about a foot and said, "Looking for sugar."

Tosh considered him for a moment. "You keep your sugar with the Bravecto?"

Ellery closed his eyes in pain. "No. Tosh..."

Her eyes widened in alarm. "What's in your hand?"

He expelled a long breath and held up the bottle. Tosh had to join him to read the tiny print.

"Trazodone?" She stared at him. "That damn well better be for Watson, Ellery."

Talk about awkward (and/or difficult) conversations.

"Look, Watson's a little dog. There's not enough here to do him harm. Even if I dump in the gabapentin, it's probably not going to knock him out. But it might make him sleepy. He had a-a strenuous night. He's going to need to crash soon."

After a moment, Tosh said, "We're not talking about Watson, are we?"

"You know we're not."

Tosh smacked the counter and then glowered up at the ceiling. "*No*. No, you're wrong. This is all Lenny and Flip. They've got this crazy idea—and by the way, they're not being very subtle about it!"

That was exactly what Ellery was afraid of, and why he felt it was imperative to act.

"Tosh—"

"Ell, you're not thinking this through. We all heard her scream seconds before we came out of our rooms. Freddie was *right there*. He couldn't have killed Chelsea in the library and made it back upstairs in thirty seconds. He wasn't even out of breath! And he'd have been covered in blood, wouldn't he?"

The fact that she had thought this through, worked it out, was significant in itself.

Ellery said, "He'd have had to kill her earlier during the night."

"We'd have heard it!"

"Not necessarily. You can't hear anything in the library from upstairs. Besides, she might not have had time to scream."

"We *heard* her scream."

"We heard what sounded like a woman's scream."

"Exactly."

Ellery trilled very softly, "Yodel-Ay-Ee-Oooo..."

Tosh gasped. Her expression was stricken.

"What are you two whispering about?" Freddie asked from the doorway.

Tosh and Ellery both jumped as if they'd been shot, and in those seconds of terrified discovery, Ellery learned that while he could not act his way out of a paper bag to save his *own* life, he was Lawrence Olivier when it came to protecting his friends.

He casually set Watson's tranquilizers on the counter next to the sugar bowl, swept all the doggie paraphernalia back into the drawer, and slid the drawer shut.

"We're arguing over who gets the last of the Frangelico," he said.

"That's easy." Freddie joined them. "The three people who know you still *have* Frangelico." He winked.

Tosh laughed and banged her shoulder into his bicep. "Typical Freddie."

Ellery moved to the fridge and unhurriedly removed the Bailey's. He glanced at Freddie, who was studying Tosh with an odd little smile. "Freddie, you've got to be freezing in your shorts."

Tosh shivered. "I know I am."

"Then why don't you and Flip and Lenny go upstairs and get dressed? Freddie and I can wait and go up when you guys get back."

Freddie listened to this with, what Ellery couldn't help thinking, was unusual attention. But then he shrugged. "Good idea. But leave your doors open so you can hear each other at all times."

"Right." Tosh gave Ellery an unreadable look before leaving the kitchen.

Ellery poured the last of the Frangelico into three of the Irish coffee mugs, and reached for the Bushmills.

"You really *do* put Frangelico in Irish coffee," Freddie observed.

"Technically, it's a Nutty Irishman. But yep."

"Interesting. So, what were you and Tosh *really* talking about? Because you both looked guilty as hell."

Ellery grimaced, said glibly, "About whether there are spyholes as well as secret passages in this house, and whether Edwin Dolph is watching right now. You scared the heck out of us."

Freddie looked surprised and then laughed. "I bet. *Are* there spyholes?"

"Not that I know of. But then I didn't know about the passageways until a couple of weeks ago."

Freddie nodded, said abruptly, "When does Jack think he's going to get his team out here?"

How to answer that? Was it to their advantage if Freddie thought he had plenty of time to do...whatever? Or was it safer to make him believe Jack was on approach? Or did it matter either way? Because if Freddie believed he was safely in the clear...

Ellery opted for honesty. "He couldn't give me an ETA. He said clearing the road to get to us is top priority, but they've still got to contend with whatever the road conditions are now. And another storm is moving in."

"*Another* storm?"

Ellery nodded, slowly measured out the Bailey's. He just needed thirty seconds or so on his own. If he could get Freddie to step into the hall to listen for what might be happening upstairs... But on what pretext?

He was starting to fear that Freddie suspected something was up.

But maybe that was his own guilty conscience.

Freddie picked up one of the little bottles Ellery had set to the side. "What's the trazodone for?"

Ellery's heart stopped. He glanced over, said guilelessly, "Gabapentin and trazodone. The vet prescribed them for Watson. Because of the Fourth of July fireworks. He's been so agitated; I was thinking I'd use them to calm him down."

Watson, sitting next to his bowl in hopes that Ellery might forget he'd already fed him, missed his cue entirely. He gazed soulfully up at them, the very picture of a pup patiently waiting in line to receive his angel wings.

"He seems okay to me."

"That's what Tosh said." Ellery shrugged. "We'll see how he does."

Enter stage right: Tosh poked her head in the kitchen doorway, and said, "The upstairs is all yours, gents!"

Ellery didn't think he imagined Freddie's controlled start.

It seemed they were *all* a little jumpy.

"That was fast," Freddie said. "Were you racing to get back down here?"

"Are you joking? We sure were. It's creepy as a tomb up there. No offense, Ellery."

"None taken. Horror movie set was the very look we were going for." It took all Ellery's will power not to look at the pill containers. He hesitated.

Was there any possible way—

"I can finish up in here," Tosh said cheerfully. "Do I need to do more than add the coffee?"

He would have to try later. Assuming Tosh didn't flush the pills down the sink to prevent him.

"Nope," Ellery said with equally fake cheeriness. "Just add coffee." He moved toward the door, Freddie right behind him.

"**W**hy do you think Chelsea went downstairs last night?" Freddie asked as they reached the top landing.

Ellery glanced at his profile. "I don't know. I guess she couldn't sleep. What I really don't understand is why she went into that passageway."

"Maybe she was looking for something."

As Ellery's eyes met Freddie's he felt an icy foreboding slither down his spine. Freddie's eyes were the eyes of a stranger. Dark and blank.

Ellery managed a laugh. "Like what? The Dourdos Aquamarine?"

Freddie blinked. "The what?"

"Remember? It's the prevailing theory of why Edwin Dolph came back to the island. To find the Dourdos Aquamarine."

Freddie said slowly, "Oh. Yeah. Hidden jewels."

"You're leaving your door open, right?" Ellery asked briskly.

Again, Freddie was momentarily confused.

"Your room door. While we change," Ellery prompted.

"Oh. Right."

Ellery's heart was pounding as he turned toward his room.

He thinks I know something. He's not sure. It's instinct.

The same instinct that was liable to warn him Ellery was becoming a threat.

What was Freddie liable to do about that? The question dogged Ellery as he scrambled into his clothes, trying to calculate his next possible move in what was beginning to feel like a game he and Freddie were playing.

A very dangerous game.

He found a small screwdriver in his nightstand and tucked it in his back pocket, and then began to second guess himself. He was genuinely afraid, yet he still felt ridiculous arming himself against *Freddie*.

That's how Noah would have felt, too.

What did you know, Noah?

What secret would Freddie have been so desperate to hide that he had been willing to kill? Not just once, *twice*.

But no. Because Chelsea's death *had* to have resulted from her figuring out that Freddie had killed Noah. She had seen something in Tosh's photos that no one else had.

Ellery glanced automatically at the rug covering the trap door of the hidden cupboard where he'd stashed Tosh's photos.

What had Chelsea seen in those faded snapshots?

And how had Freddie realized that Chelsea knew something she shouldn't? Had Chelsea *told* him? Why would she?

"Knock-knock." Freddie rapped on the door frame of Ellery's room.

"Ready," Ellery jerked out.

Freddie followed him down the staircase in silence, and with each step, Ellery wondered if his old friend might decide to give him a push and then claim he'd slipped.

He tried to reassure himself that Freddie couldn't be sure that he—that any of them—suspected him. Any more than Ellery could be sure Freddie suspected *him*.

They reached the bottom step safely, turned, still weirdly silent, and walked down the length of the great hall, into the drawing room.

Great-aunt Eudora gazed thoughtfully down from her portrait above the fireplace. Someone had started a fire in the grate and set up the gameboard for Clue on a nearby table. No one was playing, but Lenny and Flip sat at the table, drinking their coffees.

"Your coffee's here, Ell," Flip said casually. "Who do you want to be? Lenny is Miss Scarlet."

"Of course, she is." Ellery took his place beside Lenny. She patted his knee as if he'd just put his team in the lead by executing a triple back flip on the parallel bars. "I'll be Professor Plum."

"Okay, I'm Colonel Mustard."

Ellery took a swallow of coffee. It was very sweet. Briefly, he wondered if Tosh had turned the tables on him and laced *his* drink with the tranquilizers.

But no. Tosh might flush the pills down the sink. She wouldn't drug him. She had made her views on drugging *anybody* very clear.

Tosh, seated on the loveseat next to Oscar, said, "I'm guarding your coffee from Oscar, Freddie." She made a face at Oscar.

Oscar, idly, absently slipping his lucky gold coin through his long, graceful fingers, shook his head. "I don't know if I need booze in my coffee. I'm ready to fall asleep as it is."

"How in the heck can you sleep with everything going on?" Lenny inquired.

Oscar said defensively, "Nothing's going on right *now*. I didn't sleep much last night. You can only go so long on adrenaline."

Ellery watched the fluid, rhythmic motion of the gleaming coin gliding smoothly from fingertip to fingertip, rolling over Oscar's knuckles with practiced ease. As the coin disappeared from sight, Ellery had a sudden flash of memory.

And with that memory came sickening realization. He understood why Noah had known his upcoming conversation with Freddie would be a difficult one. And why Freddie, ambitious and egotistical, used to everything always going his way, had seen Noah as an unexpected and intolerable obstacle.

An obstacle to be removed from Freddie's path by whatever means necessary.

Freddie regarded Tosh for a moment and said abruptly, "I'm going to get a glass of water."

Tosh's smile faltered. Freddie turned, left the room. They listened in silence to his footsteps going down the hall.

Tosh grew very pale.

Oscar said quietly, "Holy... What does he think?"

Flip was looking pointedly at Ellery.

Ellery shook his head.

Flip opened his mouth, but Freddie was already back. He couldn't have done more than walk to the kitchen, verify the pills were still on the counter, and walk back.

Freddie said with unnerving good cheer, "Actually, I think I *will* have that coffee. I haven't had Irish coffee in years."

Nobody moved.

"Lenny, Miss Scarlet's always first," Ellery prompted.

"Not my first murder, thank you." Lenny heard herself and swallowed. She hastily rolled the dice.

Freddie picked up his mug. "Ellery says another storm is moving in," he announced.

This was met with the delight one would expect.

Oscar's fingers closed on the doubloon. His head fell back and he woke himself up with a little splutter.

"Where's Watson?" Ellery asked in quick alarm, looking around the room.

"Right here." Tosh nodded downwards, and Ellery relaxed at the sight of Watson comfortably wedged on the loveseat between Tosh and Oscar. "Our little chaperone."

"Ha," Freddie said, and sipped his Irish coffee. His brows rose. "Not bad."

After that, no one had much to say.

Five minutes passed.

Oscar and Watson dozed, Tosh stared out the window, Freddie stared at Tosh.

Ten minutes passed.

Lenny, Flip, and Ellery continued their game.

"Miss Scarlet in the kitchen with the poker," Ellery guessed.

Miss Scarlet laughed in his face.

Fifteen minutes passed.

The clocks in the hall and on the mantel soothingly ticked out each and every minute. An eternity of minutes.

Maybe Jack was already on his way. Maybe he'd be showing up with the cavalry any minute.

Eventually, Freddie placed his empty glass on the table and sat back. He closed his eyes.

Flip, Lenny, and Ellery met each other's eyes.

Freddie had had an exhausting night. Maybe all they had to do was stay quiet and still and hopefully Freddie would forget all about them.

Sure.

Freddie's eyes flew open. He wiped his hand across his face.

No one said anything. They remained motionless, watchful and silent, as Freddie's eyes flickered shut again.

Ellery glanced at Tosh. Her lips were parted.

Freddie's head fell back, his mouth fell open, and he began to snore.

CHAPTER TWENTY

Ellery stood up slowly, reaching for the poker next to fireplace. Lenny and Flip also rose, warily watching Freddie. Oscar jumped up from the sofa, and went to check Freddie, who continued to snore peacefully in his chair.

Tosh gulped, "It's okay. I crushed up the sleeping pills in the guest bathroom."

Ellery said, "The sleeping pills that are three years out of date? How many did you use?"

"How many were in the box?"

Ellery gaped at her.

"I couldn't use the trazodone. He saw you set those containers to the side." Tosh shook her head. "I could see that he knew exactly what you were planning. And if that was true, I knew that you...you must be right." She wiped hastily at the glitter forming in the corners of her eyes.

"I can't believe it," Oscar said. "*Freddie*. He's always been such a great guy. *Why*? Why would he do it?"

"There had to be something in your photos, Tosh," Flip said. "Chelsea saw it. And Freddie knew she'd seen it."

Tosh looked up. "*No*. That's what you don't understand. Freddie and I pored over those photos dozens of times when we were together. There's nothing there. Nothing incriminating. It *can't* have been the photos."

"But why else?" Flip and Lenny looked at each other.

Oscar said, "Then Chelsea really did take your photos because she was obsessed with Freddie?"

Ellery said slowly, "In a way, yes. She was bluffing. She pretended there was something in those photos. Something no one else had noticed. And because Freddie *was* guilty, he was afraid she was right."

"But why would she do that?" Tosh protested. "If she knew—are we talking about Noah? If she knew Freddie was responsible, why would she have hidden it?"

"Oh, come *on*," Oscar said. "Now he's a mass murderer? You guys. Get a grip!"

"Not a mass murderer," Ellery said. "He might not even have planned to kill Noah. It might have just been a crime of opportunity. And Chelsea happened strictly because she was somehow threatening him."

"But that doesn't fit," Lenny argued. "Chelsea was crazy about Freddie. I wouldn't be surprised if she knew about Noah the whole time. She wouldn't have threatened him. They were together the night before."

Flip regarded Ellery. "I guess it depends on what you mean by *threaten*?"

"Exactly," Ellery said. "Chelsea *was* obsessed with Freddie. But she was also really unhappy with her career and her life, and Freddie *had* offered to help her. What if she convinced herself that she could get everything she wanted through Freddie, *including* Freddie—that he might even be all for that?"

"Freddie wasn't in love with her," Tosh said with absolute certainty.

"Okay, but if he wasn't, she could remind him that maybe he owed her something? She wouldn't think of it as threatening him."

"She'd see it as sweetening the pot," Flip agreed.

"And really, whether Freddie believed her or not about the photos, from the point Chelsea started hinting about whatever it was she thought she knew, he'd start to see her as a problem that needed to be solved ASAP."

"Do you hear yourselves?" Oscar said. "Freddie killed Chelsea because she knew he killed Noah. *Why? Why* would he kill Noah? On impulse or otherwise? The police ruled it a hit-and-run."

"Because Noah knew that Freddie was the dorm sneak thief."

Ellery's friends stared at him with a mix of expressions. 'I mean, that's my guess," he said a little wearily.

Oscar said, "And that's all it is. A wild guess, Ell."

Tosh groaned and put her face in his hands. "God. He's right."

"He's *right*?" Oscar echoed.

Tosh lowered her hands. "I found it. Your lucky gold piece, when I was going through Freddie's jeans for the laundry. When we all still lived at Third Avenue North. I asked him about it, and he said he'd picked it up in the grass and was going to give it back to you. Which he did. But I had a funny feeling about it because that was like a week after you'd lost it. Except, I couldn't believe the thief was Freddie. And then we moved from the dorm and we never had another problem with anyone stealing anything."

Lenny said, "But Freddie had plenty of money. His parents were rich."

"No, they weren't." Tosh sighed. "Freddie liked that image, but back then he was strapped for cash like everyone else."

Ellery said to Oscar, "Is he breathing okay?"

Oscar studied Freddie. He nodded. "He's fine. He's out."

"Yeah, but I don't want to trust expired sleeping pills to keep him that way. I think there's rope in the garden shed."

Flip said, "I'll go with you."

"No, that's okay. If he comes to—"

"Oh. Right," Flip said quickly, with an uneasy glance at Freddie's slumped figure.

Ellery left the drawing room, and Watson abandoned his comfortable space on the sofa to follow.

In the hall, Ellery hurriedly shrugged into his parka, opened the door, and stepped outside. The air was as cold and sharp as a dip in the ocean. However, the sun was shining, and between patchy black-edged clouds, the sky was a deep and dazzling blue.

He was no expert, but it sure looked like the blizzard had passed.

Watson jumped off the steps into snow that was now much harder and icier than even the day before. Ellery waded after. As they started toward the back of the house, the distinct growl of an engine floated in the vast white silence.

Watson stopped bounding through the drifts, staring in apparent and delighted disbelief at the tiny vehicle trundling their way. He began to wag his tail.

An SUV with the blue and gold insignia of Pirate's Cove Police Department plowed up the long drive, tires spraying showers of snow.

"Thank God."

Ellery's heart lifted. Sure, it could always be Detective George Lansing to the rescue, but he knew with certainty it was Jack.

Watson knew, too, and heralded the joyous arrival for all the island to hear.

ARF! ARF! ARF!

Ellery reversed course, slogging back toward the front of the house. He reached the courtyard a full minute before the SUV, carrying an indignant Watson safely out of range, as the SUV half-slid to a stop.

Watson shoved free of Ellery with a final *how-very-dare-you* wriggle, as the driver's door opened and Jack got out. His eyes were very bright; his expression, hard with worry.

Ellery came to meet him in a kind of full-body slam. Jack's arms locked around him. Ellery's arms wrapped tightly around Jack.

"Are you okay?" Jack demanded. "You're not hurt?" He examined Ellery's face intently, closed his eyes in quick relief, and kissed him.

"I'm okay," Ellery gasped, when he could. "We're all okay. What are you doing here, Jack? How did you get through?"

"If you think I listened to that interview with Lenny and thought, *Oh hey, they're good. They can wait till the snow melts...*"

Ellery laughed shakily. "We've had quite a morning. We had to drug Freddie with sleeping pills."

"W-W-What?"

"The situation was deteriorating rapidly. Freddie knew that *we* knew, and he was trying to decide what to do about it—and us."

Jack was clearly still processing. "So, you drugged him? *You* drugged him?"

Ellery said, "I tried. Tosh finally managed it."

"You...tried..."

They were interrupted as the passenger doors of the SUV popped open and two gnomes tumbled out. They plopped into the snow.

"What in tarnation!" huffed the gnome in the lime-green parka with the pink toque.

The gnome in the navy-blue hooded parka attempted to come to her rescue, and they clutched each other like first time skaters in an ice rink.

"*Nora*?" Ellery said in wonder. "You brought Nora—and Kingston?"

"*Brought* them?" Jack repeated. "You think this was my idea?"

"The moment I heard of that poor girl's murder, I—we—knew we had to come," Nora explained earnestly. "It's so difficult to be on guard with people you care for. Those early friendships mean so much. And you're such a loyal and kind-hearted young man,"

"I'm not feeble-minded! You shouldn't have risked your life, Nora! Or Kingston's."

"Pshaw." Nora steadied herself on the hood of the SUV. "There was no real risk. To *us*."

Kingston cleared his throat, apologetically meeting Ellery's gaze.

"There most certainly was," Jack exclaimed. "I can't believe a woman of your intelligence—or a man of your age, Peabody—could use such poor judgment. If I hadn't come along when I did, you two would be ice sculptures right now."

"*Nora*," Ellery protested.

"They were broken down on the side of the road. They'd been there for hours."

Nora seemed to consider this a point in their favor. "Yes. We left the minute we heard of that poor girl's death."

Ellery said, "But how would you even know about that when everyone's stuck at home?"

Jack muttered, "I'm starting to suspect she's got the police station bugged."

Watson, who had tired of waiting for his idol to acknowledge his presence, gave up barking and launched himself at Jack and Ellery.

At the same moment, Jack and Ellery let go of each other and turned to help Nora and Kingston, so Watson hurtled right between them and cannonballed into Nora. She went down with a little squeak, taking Kingston with her.

Jack gave a funny, smothered laugh, met Ellery's startled gaze, and they hurriedly lifted Ellery's would-be rescuers to their feet, brushed them off, and ushered them to the front steps.

Ellery shoved open the front door and Watson led the way down the great hall, foretelling the glorious news to all.

Jack's arrival was greeted with huge relief by Ellery's friends.

Even the information that Jack was without backup didn't shake their confidence that everything was again under control. Which was certainly how Ellery felt.

Having verified that everyone was unhurt, Jack took a good look at Freddie, still sprawled and unconscious in his chair. He checked Freddie's pulse. He lifted a heavy eyelid, listened to Freddie's breathing—and then he handcuffed him.

Freddie slept peacefully on.

Jack departed to view the crime scene first-hand.

When he returned to the drawing room, he said sternly, "For the record, drugging someone without their knowledge is considered a serious crime. It's typically charged as a felony and can result in severe penalties, including significant prison time."

Nora and Kingston, huddled in blankets by the fireplace, looked at each other in alarm—who had *they* drugged lately?—as did Lenny and Flip. Tosh gulped. Oscar put his arm around her shoulders.

But mostly Jack was talking to Ellery, and Ellery, responded, "These weren't normal circumstances. We thought our lives were in danger—and I *still* think our lives were in danger."

Jack softened slightly. "Self-defense is a recognized legal defense, provided you have reason to believe you're in imminent danger of harm *and* your response is proportionate to the threat. However, administering sleeping pills as a preemptive measure or indirect form of self-defense, complicates the situation."

Meeting the accusing circle of stares, he added, "This isn't my personal take on the situation. This is the argument Ames' defense team is going to present. I'm giving you a heads up. But also, I want to make it clear that this is not something you can make a habit of."

Ellery said, "I'm pretty sure they don't plan on making a habit of *any* of this."

"They're not the ones I'm worried about." But there was the faintest gleam of humor in Jack's blue-green gaze.

"Oh, very funny!"

Jack was instantly back to business. "Okay, I'm going to take complete statements from each of you. I know it's too late to ask you not to discuss the case, but please don't share what transpires during our interview. Fair enough?"

Nods all around.

Don't hold your breath, Ellery thought.

"Tosh, I'm going to start with you."

Tosh lifted her chin, nodded, and led the way to the kitchen. Jack followed.

As their footsteps faded down the hall, Flip looked at Ellery. "Another game of Clue, Professor Plum?"

Ellery glanced at Freddie. Freddie's chest peacefully rose and fell. "Clue it is."

Freddie woke while Jack was finishing up his interview with Lenny.

Lifting his head, Freddie licked his lips and blinked at Nora and Kingston, now seated across from him. He frowned. Wiped his eyes. Shook his head. Peered doubtfully at Nora and Kingston again.

"Welcome back," Ellery said.

Freddie turned his head to stare at him. He lifted his wrists and studied the handcuffs. "I guess Jack's home?"

"Yep. He's interviewing everybody. You're next."

Freddie sighed, settled back in the chair. "It doesn't matter. What was I going to do? Kill *all* of my friends? It's not like I could get away with it."

A shocked silence followed.

"Nice," Flip said.

"We don't understand why you killed any of them," Ellery said.

Freddie ignored him, gazing at Tosh. "Really, Tosh? *You* drugged me?"

Tosh stared back stonily. "*Really*, Freddie?"

Freddie made a face, glanced at Ellery. "For the record, I never wanted to kill anyone."

"And yet, you did."

Freddie did not deny it. He stared out the window. Snow was melting from the roof in great wet dollops.

He said finally, "It feels like such a long time ago."

"Not to Noah's parents, I bet. It won't to Chelsea's."

Freddie exhaled a long, weary breath. "Yeah. Well, I didn't plan any of this."

"*Why?*" Tosh burst out. "Why, Freddie?"

Freddie shook his head. "I don't know. That's the truth."

"How can it be the truth? You *killed* two people!"

Freddie said slowly, "Noah, that really *was* an accident. I was driving home that night; I saw him crossing the street... He'd told me the day before that he knew I'd been stealing money and stuff when we all lived on campus. I hadn't taken anything since, but he had it in his head that I needed to pay everybody back. I mean, I *couldn't*. I didn't *have* it. And if he'd gone to the dean or something, I'd have been *out*. I'd have been *ruined*."

"So, you ran him down?" Ellery said. It was not a question. "You murdered him. Because your career was more important than his life?"

Freddie looked at him in protest. "It didn't feel like that. It wasn't a conscious thought. It was weird. I was thinking about him and then he was right in front of me. I suddenly saw how easy it would be. And it was. In fact, it was like it was supposed to happen, because he hit my windshield and cracked it, but it already *had* a crack, so I just took it into the shop as planned." He shrugged. "That was that."

It was deathly quiet. As if everyone held their breath.

"But Chelsea knew?" Ellery prompted.

"She suspected, I guess. I don't know how. She didn't like Noah. She had a thing for him our freshman year, but he wasn't interested. I felt that she knew, but we never talked about it. It was...unspoken. I trusted her." Freddie added wryly, "Until this weekend."

Ellery asked, "What the hell *did* happen this weekend?"

"I don't know," Freddie said, and he sounded sincere. "I was actually looking forward to seeing her. And she *looked* terrific. But right away she started dropping these cryptic hints about the past, and then she came right out and said she'd noticed something in Tosh's photos, and she knew that I was responsible for Noah's accident. She said it like she was sort of kidding, but she wasn't."

Freddie read Ellery's expression, and said, "And honest to God, even that wasn't a problem because I already *planned* on helping her. I'd already promised to talk to my agent. But that wasn't enough for Chelsea. She wanted *us* to be together. She thought she could blackmail me into being with her!"

"Why didn't you just..." Tosh didn't finish the thought.

Freddie said, "I called her bluff. I said I wanted to see the photos because it wasn't true, and then I waited until she went downstairs to get them. She went into the library, she opened the secret passage, and then I waited and she didn't come out. Finally, I went into the passage, and she was just standing there holding that hatchet." He shrugged. "She'd already told me she took the hatchet as one of her stupid practical jokes. But she was upset because the photos were gone and only the hatchet was left, so she knew you guys were playing a prank on *her.*"

"Not really," Ellery said. He hadn't seen the hatchet at all.

Freddie said calmly, "And then I realized that she was literally handing me the solution to a problem *she* had created."

Ellery glanced past Freddie and saw Lenny and Jack standing in the doorway. He waited for Jack to put an end to their conversation. But Jack nodded at him.

Carry on?

Ellery said automatically, "Then what?"

Freddie shrugged. "I hit her once. She didn't even have time to yell. Then I went upstairs, quietly washed off, and waited a couple of hours. I walked over to the staircase, screamed like a girl, and waited for you all to pile out of your rooms. Which I thought was pretty clever."

"Yeah, that was pretty clever," Jack commented. "Leaving your bloody handprint on the hatchet handle, not so much."

Everyone, including Freddie jumped. Freddie turned in his chair, and protested, "Hey! You can't do that. You have to read me my rights!"

Jack said sardonically, "Unfortunately, the writers of *LAPD Blues* get a lot of stuff wrong. A confession made to a group of people in a public place where there's no reasonable expectation of privacy, grants me the right to listen in right along with everyone else. But I'll be happy to Mirandize you now..."

EPILOGUE

"**I** know you're never going to invite us back," Tosh said. "But at least let us know when and where to send the wedding gifts."

It was Monday afternoon, and Ellery and Jack were at the harbor, seeing their guests off. Lenny was popping Dramamine and washing it down with a bottle of water. Flip was saying farewell to Watson. Oscar strode up the ramp, having safely stowed Tosh's luggage and his own onboard.

"Hey," Flip said. "It's not like *we* killed anyone."

Lenny choked. "Jeez, Flip," she sputtered.

Flip shrugged, gave Watson a final pat, and rose.

Jack, his arm around Ellery, said, "You know you're all always welcome."

"I thought you were coming back next summer," Ellery protested. "I thought this was going to become a regular thing."

He took in the expressions on the faces of his friends. "Well, I mean, not *all* of it—"

Tosh laughed and hugged him. When she let go, she had tears in her eyes. "You really are a glutton for punishment, Ell."

Oscar said, "When are you guys getting married? Won't Ellery be filming on location next summer?"

"Uh, we haven't actually set the date yet," Ellery glanced at Jack.

Jack said calmly, "We should do that as soon as possible. Maybe we can squeeze in a quick honeymoon around your shooting schedule."

Remembering Jack's initial reaction to the idea of his returning to films, Ellery smiled gratefully. The corner of Jack's eyes crinkled in response.

Lenny suggested, "Maybe you can honeymoon on location."

"Not exactly what I had in mind," Ellery said. "Anyway, it's a small role. It shouldn't require more than a day or two of shooting."

"We'll work it out," Jack promised.

The Pirate Queen's horn blasted a final warning. There was another quick round of hugs and kisses, and then Tosh, Oscar, Lenny, and Flip hurried down the ramp and up the gangplank. They disappeared inside the ship and Ellery watched them moving past the windows as they made their way down the aisle, finding their seats.

He sighed. Jack gave him a little squeeze. Watson yipped in farewell.

The November wind whipped around them, kicking up whitecaps on the gray water, chilling their cheeks and ruffling their coats. Watson huddled against Ellery's legs.

From inside the main cabin, Tosh waved goodbye. Ellery waved back.

Slowly, ponderously, the *Pirate Queen* pushed back from the dock, churning the water blue-green. As the ferry turned away, her foghorn bellowed a deep, resonant farewell, the sound echoing across the water.

Jack tightened his grip on Ellery's waist, smiled down at him.

"*Theatah* people, eh?" Ellery said lightly.

"Some of my very favorite people are theater people." Jack dropped a quick kiss on Ellery's temple.

Ellery sighed, leaned his head on Jack's shoulder. They watched until the ferry shrank to a small speck against the gray horizon and was at last swallowed by the misty distance.

ABOUT THE AUTHOR

Author of over 100+ titles of Gay Mystery and M/M Romance, Josh Lanyon has built her literary legacy on twisty mystery, kickass adventure, and unapologetic man-on-man romance.

Her work has been translated into twelve languages. The FBI thriller *Fair Game* was the first Male/Male title to be published by Italy's Harlequin Mondadori and *Stranger on the Shore* (Harper Collins Italia) was the first M/M title to be published in print. In 2016 *Fatal Shadows* placed #5 in Japan's annual Boy Love novel list (the first and only title by a foreign author to place on the list). The Adrien English series was awarded the All-Time Favorite Couple by the Goodreads M/M Romance Group. In 2019, *Fatal Shadows* became the first LGBTQ mobile game created by *Moments: Choose Your Story*.

She's an EPIC Award winner, a four-time Lambda Literary Award finalist (twice for Gay Mystery), an Edgar nominee, and the first ever recipient of the Goodreads All Time Favorite M/M Author award.

Josh is married and lives in Southern California with her irascible husband, two adorable dogs, a small garden, and an ever-expanding library of vintage mystery destined to eventually crush them all beneath its weight.

Find other Josh Lanyon titles at www.joshlanyon.com

Follow Josh on Twitter, Facebook, Goodreads, Instagram and Tumblr, and for extras and exclusives, join Josh on Patreon.

ALSO BY JOSH LANYON

NOVELS

The ADRIEN ENGLISH Mysteries
Fatal Shadows • A Dangerous Thing • The Hell You Say
Death of a Pirate King • The Dark Tide
Stranger Things Have Happened • So This is Christmas
A Funny Thing Happened

The HOLMES & MORIARITY Mysteries
Somebody Killed His Editor • All She Wrote
The Boy with the Painful Tattoo • In Other Words...Murder

The ALL'S FAIR Series
Fair Game • Fair Play • Fair Chance

The ART OF MURDER Series
The Mermaid Murders •The Monet Murders
The Magician Murders • The Monuments Men Murders
The Movie-Town Murders

BEDKNOBS AND BROOMSTICKS
Mainly by Moonlight • I Buried a Witch
Bell, Book and Scandal

The SECRETS AND SCRABBLE Series
Murder at Pirate's Cove • Secret at Skull House
Mystery at the Masquerade • Scandal at the Salty Dog
Body at Buccaneer's Bay • Lament at Loon Landing
Death at the Deep Dive • Corpse at Captain's Seat

OTHER NOVELS

This Rough Magic • The Ghost Wore Yellow Socks
Mexican Heat (with Laura Baumbach) • Strange Fortune
Come Unto These Yellow Sands • Stranger on the Shore
Winter Kill • Jefferson Blythe, Esquire
Murder in Pastel • The Curse of the Blue Scarab
The Ghost Had an Early Check-out
Murder Takes the High Road • Séance on a Summer's Night
Hide and Seek • A Puzzle for Two

NOVELLAS

The DANGEROUS GROUND Series
Dangerous Ground • Old Poison • Blood Heat
Dead Run • Kick Start • Blind Side

OTHER NOVELLAS

Cards on the Table • The Dark Farewell • The Dark Horse
The Darkling Thrush • The Dickens with Love
I Spy Something Bloody • I Spy Something Wicked
I Spy Something Christmas • In a Dark Wood
The Parting Glass • Snowball in Hell • Mummy Dearest
Don't Look Back • A Ghost of a Chance
Lovers and Other Strangers • Out of the Blue
A Vintage Affair • Lone Star (in Men Under the Mistletoe)
Green Glass Beads (in Irregulars) • Blood Red Butterfly
Everything I Know • Baby, It's Cold (in Comfort and Joy)
A Case of Christmas • Murder Between the Pages
Slay Ride • Stranger in the House • The Lemon Drop Kid

SHORT STORIES

*A Limited Engagement • The French Have a Word for It
In Sunshine or In Shadow • Until We Meet Once More
Icecapade (in His for the Holidays) • Perfect Day
Heart Trouble • Other People's Weddings (Petit Mort)
Slings and Arrows (Petit Mort)
Sort of Stranger Than Fiction (Petit Mort)
Critic's Choice (Petit Mort) • Just Desserts (Petit Mort)
In Plain Sight • Wedding Favors • Wizard's Moon
Fade to Black • Night Watch • Plenty of Fish
Halloween is Murder • The Boy Next Door
Requiem for Mr. Busybody*

COLLECTIONS

*Short Stories (Vol. 1)
Sweet Spot (the Petit Morts)
Merry Christmas, Darling (Holiday Codas)
Christmas Waltz (Holiday Codas 2)
I Spy...Three Novellas
Dangerous Ground The Complete Series
Dark Horse, White Knight (Two Novellas)
The Adrien English Mysteries Box Set
The Adrien English Mysteries Box Set 2
Male/Male Mystery & Suspense Box Set
Partners in Crime (Three Classic Gay Mystery Novels)
All's Fair Complete Collection
Shadows Left Behind*